# YOUR HEART TO BREAK

## SHIRLEY SIATON

# A NOTE FOR THE READER

Thank you for picking up *Your Heart to Break: Dark Love Stories.* As the title suggests, this collection explores the intersection of love and darkness, often in intense and challenging ways. These stories delve into heavy themes, raw emotional dynamics, and feature characters who are survivors, fighters, and sometimes, villains, often making difficult choices.

While I believe deeply in the catharsis, love, and healing found within these pages, I want you to be able to make the best and safest reading choice for you. Your well-being is the most important thing.

Please be aware that this book contains the following themes and potential triggers:

- Explicit sexual content (spice)
- Major character death
- Grief, bereavement, and the death of a partner/family member
- Stalking (romantic, protective, and professional)
- Kidnapping, abduction, and non-consensual drugging
- Recounted domestic abuse and severe childhood trauma
- Vigilante justice, revenge killing, and gang violence
- Past incarceration/imprisonment
- PTSD, panic attacks, and nightmares
- On-page violence, blood, and significant injury detail
- Recounted parental suicide and accidental death
- Poverty and significant financial hardship
- Power imbalance dynamics
- Themes of abandonment and self-destructive behavior

To all my readers,
with all my heart

# CONTENTS

# YOUR HEART TO BREAK

# THE MAN IN THE SHADOWS

# CHAPTER 1

## The Crowd

I NOTICE HIM BEFORE I EVER HEAR HIS VOICE.

Megaworld on a Tuesday night is crowded, neon lights splashing the rain-soaked pavement. I'm balancing grocery bags from picking up essentials after work, irritated at myself for forgetting an umbrella, when I see him for the first time.

At first, it's a presence, a strong and undeniable pull.

Then I look toward one of the refreshment stands.

The sight of him hits me like a bolt of lightning.

He's tall—taller than most people rushing around us. He has short, neatly-styled hair, falling over a wide forehead. His shoulders and chest look impossibly broad and strong under his charcoal shirt.

But it's his eyes that hold on to me like invisible chains.

They're deep-set on his face, slightly narrowed, fixed on me like I'm the only thing worth looking at. His lips, shaped like something sensuous and sinful, curl into what could only be a smirk.

I take a deep breath. Then, with a scowl at everything and nothing at once, I rush off.

The second time, I spot him at the bus stop near Festive Walk. He doesn't even pretend to be casual.

He's just there. Waiting.

Watching.

By the third, I snap.

I march up to him outside the mall entrance, my bags cutting into my palms.

"Are you following me?" I demand without preamble.

He doesn't flinch. His mouth curves in response. His voice comes out in a measured, richly textured drawl. "Yes."

My stomach drops. "You're not even embarrassed to admit that?"

"No." His response is even, threaded with something dangerous. "I told myself I'd just watch. That it would be enough. But it isn't."

My pulse is a thunderous mess.

I glare at him. "Why me?"

"Because I saw you once and couldn't stop watching you. You were looking up at all these towers that belonged to other people, and all I could think was they should belong to you instead."

I laugh nervously, trying to think of something equally ridiculous as a clapback. "You own one of these buildings, don't you?"

His lips twitch. "Three, actually."

"Oh my God. What are you, some kind of stalker CEO?"

The words come out sounding more of a Wattpad fever dream than intended.

"Yes," he says simply. "But only yours."

I roll my eyes. "You've got to be joking."

"No, I'm not," he answers, deadpan. He inclines his head toward my bags. "Can I help you with those?"

I shake my head as I continue walking to my stop. Unfazed, he keeps up with me easily, one stride equivalent to two and a half of mine. I don't know whether to laugh or scream at the insanity of the situation.

When the bus arrives, he gestures to the black SUV parked at the curb, in one of the reserved spots that only VIPs could access. "Let me drive you home, miss."

"No, thanks," I mutter, stepping up into the bus. "I'm fine."

For a second, I think I see something flicker in his eyes.

It's definitely not anger, or even disappointment.

He just regards me patiently, then lowers his head in an exaggerated farewell nod that looks more like a knightly bow.

I don't know if I should just give in to the weakness in my knees or throw something at him. But even the canned corned beef in my reusable grocery bag is too eye-wateringly expensive to waste, especially when it will last me at least four square meals. Or six, if I can get a potato from my landlady.

But I can't take my eyes off him as he watches the bus drive off, not moving from his spot on the sidewalk.

# CHAPTER 2

## The Rain

THE NEXT TIME I SEE HIM, IT'S RAINING HEAVILY.

I leave my office and find him waiting under the awning, holding an umbrella big enough for two.

"You again," I mutter.

"Me again," he says easily. He doesn't offer excuses.

I should walk away. Run, maybe, or call our security guard at the bank. But instead I stand rooted to the pavement, fighting the wild heat churning in my stomach.

"You don't even know me," I say.

His gaze doesn't waver. "Then let me."

I meet his eyes without blinking. "I don't really know if I should."

He gestures to a coffee shop down the block. "Let me buy you coffee and something to eat. Least I could do. Catching your bus in this weather would be a nightmare."

I sigh, and nod without saying anything, knowing he's right. Inwardly, I'm berating myself for saying yes to a man who is pretty much stalking me.

We sit side by side at a corner table. The downpour

outside lashes against the glass, trapping us in a little bubble of dark and warmth.

"What's your name?" he asks.

"Thea."

"I'm Noah," he offers. The name fits him—solid, old-fashioned, biblical almost.

He stirs his black coffee without drinking it. "Tell me something real, Thea."

I can only blink at him. "What?"

"No small talk. Tell me something I shouldn't know."

I shake my head, laughing nervously as I stir my own cappuccino. "That's a lot to ask from a stranger."

"We're not strangers," he says. "Not anymore."

His intensity should unsettle me. Maybe it does. But it also draws me in, like a strong whirlwind I can't fight.

Against my better judgment, I say, "I don't go home to Negros if I can help it. My family…my father. It's very complicated."

Something flickers in his eyes. "Then don't go home. Stay where you want to stay."

"And where's that?" I challenge.

His answer is quiet, but the words are lethal. "With me."

I feel scorching heat take over my entire body, from the pit of my belly to the tips of my hair.

"Tell me something about you, too," I say, looking away so he can't see how red my face has become.

He doesn't respond at first. Instead, he reaches for my chin with his index finger, turning my head gently to look back at him.

"People stay close to the money," he says softly. "Not to me, Thea. Never for me."

Something twists in my chest. For the first time, he doesn't look mysterious and untouchable.

He looks human.

"I'm sorry," I say honestly.

"Don't be," he replies. "I've learned to read people that way. I see them coming from kilometers away."

I can only nod, watching him as he picks up his cup of coffee and takes a sip.

I finish my cappuccino in silence, too, but it's not the kind that's awkward. It's the kind of quiet that breathes and waits and doesn't ask for anything.

When we leave the coffee shop, the streets are slick with rain. The neon lights of Megaworld paint the puddles pink and gold. He walks me to the bus stop, my lunch tote in his hand, umbrella angled more over my head than his.

"You're insane, you know that?" I mutter, unable to keep from smiling like an idiot.

"Maybe." His eyes glint. "But only for you. You should know that by now."

When the bus arrives, I hesitate, caught between nerves and want, between common sense and something that feels like fate.

He leans down, voice a whisper just for me. "Tell me to stay away, Thea, and I'll disappear. You'll never see me again."

My heart races. I should say it.

But I don't.

The truth, bold and a little crazy, escapes my lips instead. "Don't you dare."

The smile that breaks over his face is enough to take my breath away.

And when he kisses me right there under the rain, softly,

almost hesitantly, the city fades until there's nothing left but the two of us.

That night, I dream of him, holding me in the dark, telling me to stay with him.

For him.

# CHAPTER 3

## The Drizzle

**I**T DRIZZLES THE FOLLOWING NIGHT.

I step out of the bank and he's there. His umbrella is tilted toward me, raindrops sliding down the sleeve of his shiny gray polo shirt.

"Didn't think you'd be here," I blurt out, heart expanding in a strange kind of relief at seeing him.

"Come on," he answers casually. "It's dinner time."

My stomach betrays me with a loud growl. He gives me a smug, knowing grin in response.

"Fine," I say. "You're buying."

He brings me to a restaurant in the mall with tall glass windows and warm lights, a place too expensive for me to ever go into on my own. It's the kind of place where the waiters seem to glide instead of walk.

The staff and some of the customers, all beautiful women and men, greet him by name.

"Is this your restaurant?" I ask, incredulous.

"One of them," he admits. "This is my youngest baby."

I shake my head, laughing softly. "Of course it is."

A statuesque woman with gray hair piled on top of her head guides us to a corner booth with velvety soft dark blue seats, then backs away gracefully after giving us shiny tablets of the menu. A minute later, a waiter who looks like J-Hope of BTS serves us glasses of iced tea, complete with lemon slices and tiny paper umbrellas.

I try not to gawk at the prices of the food and drinks. "What else do you own, then? Half of Megaworld?"

He smirks. "Only the parts worth keeping."

I snort, then cover my mouth. "Sorry. That sounded rude."

"No," he says, leaning back in his chair. "I like the way you say what you mean."

My cheeks and neck burn at his compliment, so I save face and ask him to choose for me a dish on the menu he thinks I would like best.

Noah orders chicken mushroom soup and a beetroot salad for our shared starters, then sirloin for himself and baby back ribs for me.

Over the smoothest, tastiest soup I have ever tasted, he studies me in that unblinking way he has, and it makes me spill things I never meant to.

"I grew up in Escalante City," I confess, tracing the rim of my glass. "Every fight, every slammed door, every bruise my mother tried to hide…it all felt louder there. She used to lock me in a dark room whenever my father got home drunk, telling me if I can't see anything it would make it less real. Well, I came here because…I thought if I was far enough away, maybe the sounds wouldn't follow me."

The words taste bitter, but he doesn't look away. He doesn't pity me either. He just listens.

"You've been running," he says quietly.

"Yes," I admit.

"Does it help?"

I huff out a laugh. "Some days. I do my best."

When the main course arrives, he surprises me by offering his plate first. It's a thick, juicy cut of steak. "I got the recipe from a pit master in Arizona. He uses ground coffee beans along with other spices to rub onto the meat. Try it."

I stare at him. "You don't strike me as the sharing type."

"Maybe only when it's you," he says, and it's so blunt my fork tumbles over the ribs on my plate, soaking the handle in sauce.

He chuckles at my expression, then sobers. "I've been alone for a while too. Different reason. My parents separated long before all this. Other people…well, they like to know what I own, not who I am."

"Who are you, then?" I ask before I can stop myself.

His gaze pins me where I sit. "That depends. Who do you need me to be?"

My chest tightens. I look down at my plate, pretending my heart isn't hammering.

"You can't just…say things like that," I mutter.

"I just did." His voice is calm, but there's something beneath it, something dark and unhesitating.

I look back up at him. "I need you to be who you are to me."

"And what's that, Thea?"

"Someone honest. Someone who's not afraid to step out of the dark and tell me things other people try not to say."

He raises an eyebrow, the corner of his mouth quirking

in a half-smile. "I've already done that. Surprises me you're still here, actually, in spite of it."

I reach across and tap his nose with my index finger. "You have no idea, Mr. CEO. You don't even know what you've gotten yourself into."

That makes him laugh, a rich, rolling sound that rumbles off his chest and makes me smile right back.

By dessert, a large bowl of *crème brûlée* that J-Hope serves with two golden teaspoons, I'm giggling despite myself. Noah tells me about nearly burning down a kitchen in a hotel in Los Angeles when he was eighteen. I admit I once stole mangoes from my neighbor's tree and blamed it on the cat, then at the typhoon.

For a moment, it feels normal. Just a man and a woman sharing a meal. A very expensive one, but still.

As we get ready to leave, Noah leans in, voice quiet but unshakable. "Don't mistake this for coincidence, Thea. I'm not here by accident."

And I believe him.

The rain has stopped by the time he pulls up the SUV outside my boardinghouse in Mandurriao.

It's the kind of place you only live in if you're desperate: peeling paint, tiny rooms, the echo of other people's arguments through thin walls. I expect him to make a face or make a comment.

He doesn't.

Instead, he kills the engine of his car and steps out to open my door. My shoes squelch against the wet pavement, and suddenly I feel small beside him—me in my white-collar uniform and department store footwear, him in a sleek jacket that probably costs more than six months' rent.

At the gate, he pauses and takes my hand. His grip is warm and steady.

"You need anything?" His thumb brushes my knuckles like it's a habit already.

I shake my head too quickly. "No."

Something changes in his eyes. It's neither disappointment nor acceptance, but something sure, almost determined. But he doesn't say anything.

Instead, he bends and presses his lips to the back of my hand. A kiss so old-fashioned, my knees nearly buckle.

"Goodnight, Thea."

My voice is a shaky whisper when I answer. "Goodnight."

I slip inside the gate, but I look back. He's still there, leaning against his SUV, watching. I raise my hand in a small wave. He lifts his in return, slowly.

Neighbors gather at their gates and peek out of their windows, whispering behind their hands. Eyes flick from me to Noah's car and back again.

I ignore them. My pulse is still caught in my hand where his mouth touched.

I watch him back the car out of the narrow street, then wave again just before he drives off into the night.

I know exactly what I need, but I couldn't tell him.

Because it's him.

# CHAPTER 4

## The Blackout

IT RAINS HARDER THE NEXT DAY.

My colleagues chat idly during coffee breaks about another typhoon coming in, this time stronger than the one that hit Iloilo less than a month ago.

By the time evening comes, sheets of water blur the streetlights, turning the city into liquid glass.

When I step out of my office after a month-end closing that feels dragged out, I see Noah's SUV parked outside the bank.

This time, he doesn't even ask. He just gets out, umbrella already open, hand outstretched for me.

I take it. This time, he kisses me on the cheek.

He takes me to another restaurant, different from last night's. The other place—his "oldest baby"—is smaller and more intimate, tucked into a quiet corner near the Esplanade. Despite the weather, the other tables are occupied by couples, all speaking in whispers over their drinks.

I watch the soft golden lights flicker against the glass as

rain streaks down the windowpanes. Seated from across me, he reaches out and takes my hand.

"Yes?" I ask, trying to cover the nervous flutter in my chest.

"You're so beautiful," he says.

I roll my eyes, but my face is hot.

"I'm not kidding," he insists. "This is how I first saw you, you know. It was around sunset. You were looking at my building. The light hit the glass, and then it fell on you. You looked like you glowed—no, you looked like you're fire itself."

I can only shake my head, unable to speak.

"You weren't even looking at me, Thea," he continues, his eyes locked onto mine. "You were looking at the glass and the light and the shadows, but I wanted you to look at me like that. I was going to give you all the towers you wanted just so I can see you looking like fire."

"I'm sure you're disappointed," I manage to say, keeping my voice light.

"Disappointed?" he echoes, chuckling. "Quite the opposite. I got exactly what I wanted."

I freeze at his words. "What do you mean? What did you want?"

Noah smiles. "I wanted someone to look at me like I'm glass and light and shadows."

"And?" I whisper.

"And you did. You do."

I nod. "Because you're all that and more. Just like me. Maybe that's why…"

"Maybe that's why we found each other?" he finishes. Something raw threads through his words.

I nod again, a lone tear sliding down my cheek.

In a split second, he's crouching next to me, pressing a gray handkerchief to my eyes.

"Don't," he murmurs, his other hand smoothing down my hair. "Don't cry. Please."

I can't look at him, so I take the handkerchief and pat away the tears. "You don't even know me."

"I know enough." His voice is low. "I know you're brave. I know you ran and you survived. I know you laugh when you don't mean to. I know you pretend you don't need help even when you do."

My throat closes. "How could you possibly know all that?"

"Because I've been watching. I've been listening to everything you say and don't say."

It should terrify me. Maybe it does. But more than anything, it makes me feel seen.

Our food arrives just in time. We eat in companionable silence, then he gently guides me to the car.

By the time the SUV rolls up to the boardinghouse, the storm has gutted the street. Every window is black, the rain hammering against the tin rooftops like heavy fists.

"There's no power," he says softly. "The rain must have knocked it out."

Noah is out of the car the moment he shuts off the engine. He takes the umbrella from the back seat and moves to the passenger side. The air feels heavy as I step out onto the flooded pavement. The neighbors have all retreated indoors, the faint glow of lamps and candles flickering dimly behind shutters and curtains.

He guides me through the gate, the beam of his phone

torch barely cutting through the dark. We step inside the narrow hallway together.

I feel the shadows close in. The water dripping from my jacket onto the cracked tiles feels like a roaring sea instead of a puddle.

My chest feels tight. Too tight.

At my door, I fumble with the keys. My hand is shaking. The darkness presses too tightly.

"Noah," I whisper. My throat feels raw and dry. "Don't…"

He moves closer. "Don't what?"

My voice cracks when I answer. "Don't leave me in the dark."

For a heartbeat, the space between us roars louder than the rain outside. Then something in him breaks free.

He takes my face in his hand, tilts it up, and kisses me.

It isn't tentative. It's fire.

It's our restraint breaking like glass.

His mouth moves against mine with raw hunger, but his hand stays gentle, thumb stroking my cheek as though I'll shatter.

I gasp, and he swallows the sound, pressing me back against the door. My keys slip from my fingers and clatter to the floor. I don't care.

My fists bunch in his damp shirt, pulling him close, needing him closer. His body is all strength, steady and unyielding, the kind of weight that feels like safety instead of danger.

"Thea," he rasps between kisses, cheek pressed to mine, breath hot on my skin. "Say no, and I'll leave. Just one word."

"Don't go," I whisper desperately. "Please don't go."

Lightning splits the sky outside, throwing his face into

sharp relief. For a split second, I can see the wet hair plastered to his forehead, the hunger in his eyes, the fierce tenderness he's trying and failing to hold back.

He groans low in his throat, then his arms are around me, lifting me like I weigh nothing. My legs wrap around his waist instinctively. The movement knocks a breathless laugh out of me before his mouth steals it.

Everywhere he touches ignites. My back. My hips. The curve of my thigh. His hands are careful, but the tension in his grip tells me he's holding back more than I can imagine.

"You're mine," he murmurs against my ear, the words almost lost to the thunder. "You don't have to be afraid anymore."

I bury my face against his shoulder, trembling from the flood of want rushing through me like the downpour outside. "Then don't let me go. Stay in the dark with me."

His answer is another kiss, deeper and hungrier, one that leaves me breathless and aching and certain.

The wind howls. The boardinghouse creaks. But for the first time in years, the dark feels like shelter.

Because Noah is in it with me.

And when he carries me out of the hallway, I don't care where we end up.

As long as I'm still in his arms.

# CHAPTER 5

## The Promise

**H**IS APARTMENT SMELLS OF MINT AND COFFEE.

I barely remember him carrying me to the car and driving off. He doesn't stop driving until we reach a high-rise condominium building, where he parks underground and carries me into the elevator.

As we enter his penthouse unit, warm light spills from a single lamp, falling on steel and glass fixtures. Dark couches and cushions that look impossibly soft form a circle in the middle of the room.

I've barely stepped inside before Noah's arm goes around my waist. His touch feels like he's been holding this back for far too long.

"Are you sure?" he asks me softly.

"I'm sure," I answer, leaning against him. "I want this. With you."

Something in his eyes shatters. The next second, he's kissing me. It's not a careful brush but a deep, hungry drag of his mouth over mine, his palm cupping my jaw. My hands slide up his chest, fingers clutching at his shirt. I can feel his control like a tremor under his skin.

He breaks the kiss just enough to murmur against my lips, "I'll stop if you want me to."

"I don't want you to stop," I breathe, my whole body shaking. "Please, Noah."

The sound he makes is raw and guttural, then he's pressing me against the cool wall. His mouth trails down my throat, his teeth grazing just enough to make me gasp. His hands settle on my hips, lifting me so my toes leave the floor, my skirt riding up. The power of it steals my breath.

"You're mine, Thea," he rasps against my neck. "Tonight and every night after. I'll take very good care of you. I promise."

"Yes," I whisper. "Please."

He curses under his breath. Then his hands are on my thighs, dragging them around his waist. He lifts me and carries me across the hall and into the bedroom, setting me on the edge of the large white mattress. He kneels in front of me, fingers tracing the inside of my knees, his eyes dark and searching.

"I'm going to touch you," he says quietly. "I'm going to make you feel good. And if it's too much, tell me."

I nod, biting my lip, and his mouth finds mine again. He goes slow at first, coaxing and guiding. His hands slide up under my damp blouse, skimming my ribs, pausing just below my breasts. He watches my face, waiting. When I arch into his palms, he groans and covers my skin fully, thumbs circling my nipples through my bra.

Then he kisses me.

This time, it's rough, hungry. He presses me back onto

the bed, his body caging mine, his mouth trailing down to my collarbone, biting and sucking lightly, then soothing with his tongue until I'm trembling beneath him. His hands are already at the waistband of my skirt, tugging it down inch by inch, his fingers grazing my thighs with every movement. Then he unbuttons and slides my blouse off, followed quickly by my bra.

"You're so beautiful," he growls, nuzzling each breast in turn. "So fucking beautiful."

I shudder, reaching for him as he licks and sucks my nipples, and the world narrows to the press of his weight, the heat of his breath, the sound of rain against the window.

He kisses down my stomach, then looks up at me from between my thighs.

"You're shaking," he murmurs.

"It just that…I haven't done this before."

He pauses for a moment, then kisses my inner thigh. "Then let me show you what it means to be wanted."

He peels my panties down and slides them off with agonizing care. Then his mouth is on me, scorching hot, his tongue circling slow and low. I cry out, startled, my hips lifting off the bed.

"Easy," he murmurs against me. "Let me."

He eats like a man starved. His hands grip my thighs, holding me wide and open, and I feel everything. Every drag of his tongue, every groan he gives when I tremble, every low curse when I gasp out his name.

When he finally pulls away, I'm dazed and panting hard. My legs fall apart, shameless and wanting. He doesn't take his eyes off me as he unbuttons his shirt, then pushes down his dark slacks and briefs in one smooth motion.

Finally, he stands naked before me.

And my God, he does.

His body is corded with muscle, like carved marble beneath brown velvet, from his impossibly wide shoulders and chest tapering to narrow hips and strong, lean legs.

Between them, I see all of *him*.

He's big. Hard. Thick enough to make my breath catch.

His jaw clenches as he watches my face.

"I'll go slow," he says, voice tight. "I'll never hurt you. You know that, right?"

I nod, then say, "I want you too."

I rise from the bed, bare and trembling, alive in a way I don't have words for. He watches me with fire in his eyes, but he doesn't move. He just breathes, shoulders tense, like he's holding himself back for my sake.

That restraint undoes me more than anything else.

I move toward him on my knees, my pulse slamming against my throat. I reach out and touch him, the muscles of his stomach tight and trembling under my fingers. I rest a hand on his thigh and feel the jolt that goes through him.

"I want to taste you," I whisper.

He blinks hard. "Fuck, Thea..."

"I need to."

Then I lower my mouth. I take a deep breath, and slide him between my lips.

His hand flies to my hair. He lets out a moan that's half agony, half pleasure.

I take my time. I explore him like my own delicious secret. I don't really know what I'm doing, but I want to learn. I want to know how to make him fall apart.

And somehow, I do. I pump him in and out of my mouth.

I cradle the soft weight of his balls between my hands as I suck. I feel his hips buckling, his hands pulling at my hair, as he swears and mutters my name.

"Stop," he growls. "Stop. You're gonna make me come right now."

I pull back, licking my lips, stunned.

"You're shaking," I murmur breathlessly.

His eyes are almost black now. "I want it to be inside you, baby."

I nod. My body is trembling for something—and I know exactly what it is.

He pushes me back onto the bed and slides over me, eyes never leaving mine. One hand braces beside my head. The other guides himself to my entrance, where I'm wet and warm and aching for him.

"Just the tip," he says softly. "You'll tell me if it hurts."

I put my arms around his neck, settling my face against his shoulder. "I trust you."

The first press is a small burn, a stretch that makes me gasp until I almost sink my teeth into his skin. He stills instantly, a curse spilling from his mouth.

"You're so tight," he groans. "Jesus, Thea, your body's holding me like it never wants to let go."

I dig my fingers into his back. "Don't stop. Please. I want all of it."

His control fractures. He thrusts deeper, slowly, inch by inch until he's buried to the hilt. We both moan at the feeling. My body clenches around him, the fullness overwhelming, the pleasure riding on the edge of too much.

He holds still for a moment, lips in my hair, his breath coming fast.

"Fuck, you feel so perfect," he says. "You're mine now. You know that, don't you?"

I nod, tears pricking at my eyes. "Yours."

And then he moves.

Slowly at first, dragging almost all the way out before sinking back in with a shudder. But it doesn't take long before his rhythm changes, before he starts to take me in earnest, each thrust stealing my breath.

"You take it so well," he rasps. "You're so perfect, baby. So goddamn tight."

He grips my wrists and pins them above my head with one hand, his other arm anchoring me as his hips slam into mine. The bed creaks beneath us, the headboard hitting the wall with every thrust. I cry out as pleasure begins to roll around me in waves.

My back arches, and I whimper his name.

He groans, deep and guttural. "You like that? You like when I fuck you like this?"

"Yes! Oh God, yes…"

"Then take it," he growls, hips pumping faster. "Take everything. It's yours. Only yours."

My climax hits like lightning, sudden and electric. My entire body tightens around him, a resounding cry leaving my mouth.

He curses and shouts my name, crashing into his own release, hips jerking as he spills inside me, still grinding through the aftershocks as if he can't bear to leave my body.

When he finally collapses on top of me, we're both gasping and sweating.

He brushes a kiss against my cheek, then my neck, then my lips.

"You okay?" he whispers.

I nod, dizzy from pleasure, blissfully sore. "More than okay."

He cups my face, thumb brushing my lips.

"Then stay with me. Please."

I reach up and take his face in both hands, pressing my mouth to his.

"Always."

In the middle of the night, he wakes me gently, then carries me to the shower.

The water hisses to life. Steam rises around us.

Noah pins me gently to the tiles, kissing me like he needs to memorize the shape of my mouth. Then he drops to his knees.

I barely have time to gasp before his mouth is on me. The sound I make, wild and shamelessly loud, doesn't even feel like mine. One of my hands claws at the fogged glass wall, the other tangles in his hair.

I've never felt anything like this. He devours me, half-asleep and trembling, my knees draped over his shoulders.

When I come, it's like I've been broken into pieces and rebuilt all at once. I sag against him as he rises and puts his arms around my waist, kissing my shoulders, my breasts.

He turns me carefully, bracing me against the wall. His hand finds its way between my legs, stroking and petting the wetness there that has everything to do with him.

He buries his face at the back of my neck, teeth nipping softly at the skin. "Tell me you want this."

"I want this," I breathe. "I want you."

When he pushes inside me from behind, I cry out.

Not in pain. Not even in fear. In wonder.

It doesn't hurt the way I thought it would.

It feels like finding a place where I am wanted without question, where I can feel without fear.

His other hand finds my breast, the other rubs me relentlessly as he moves. I fall into the rhythm of him, mouth open, eyes closed, every breath a prayer I don't know how to say.

And when he comes inside me, when his fingers and the length of him bring me to the peak, I scream his name as we pump against each other, falling with the cresting wave that only the two of us can ride.

I hear him say it as his arms circle my waist, as he kisses my wet hair tenderly.

"I love you, baby. I love you."

# CHAPTER 6

## *The Surrender*

I DECIDE I WANT TO OWN THIS.

Noah wraps me in a towel and carries me back to the bed. Although drenched and practically boneless, I toss the towel aside and climb on top of him.

"I want to see you," I say, "from here."

I sink down just above his hips and he curses, gripping my thighs tightly. My hands cradle his face, my breasts push against his chest, and I kiss him deeply.

"You're beautiful like this," I whisper, grinding my hips against his.

I feel him stirring back to life. My body responds with the now-familiar heat pooling between my legs, ready for him once more.

"So are you," he mutters.

His hands find my breasts, rolling my nipples between his fingers. I gasp, rolling my hips in response, chasing the friction that I have come to know intimately that night.

My body burns, but in the best way.

"Say it, Noah," I tell him as I take him into my body, as

I surrender to the dark, delicious depths of the man who watched me from the shadows and, somehow, loved me.

"I love you," he growls. "I fucking love you."

I thrust my hips against his, up and down, to the music of the rain, to the sound of his curses and his gasps.

And I say it.

"I love you too."

He grins, his hands digging into my hips. "About fucking time."

I squeal as he pumps into me, and I meet him in the middle of our rhythm.

We move together, faster and harder, and I don't care if the whole damn world hears me screaming his name.

I want this carved into my memory. I want all of him carved into me.

Into the glass and the light and the shadows of me.

And as we fall together once more, it's the first time I have ever felt whole.

❧

When I wake just before dawn, it isn't in my narrow boardinghouse room.

It's in long shadows and soft sheets, in a room too big, too sleek, windows opening out to the dark city skyline blurred with rain.

Memory comes in delicious, sinful snippets that make me sink back onto the bed.

I'm at Noah's place.

The other side of the bed is empty, but on the nightstand sits a steaming cup of coffee and a note in bold handwriting.

*Stay. You're safe here.*

*Always.*

*Love, N.*

I press the note to my chest.

For the first time in my life, the dark doesn't feel like it's swallowing me whole.

Because Noah stood in it with me.

And he never let go.

# THE ROOMMATE AGREEMENT

# CHAPTER 1

## Not A Girl

**S**HE ARRIVES AT DAWN.

When I first meet Joni, she's standing in the doorway of the apartment with her arms crossed, staring at me like she's seen a ghost.

"You're…Leslie Lim?"

I nod, bleary-eyed from interrupted sleep, still exhausted from the previous day of grad school classes, teaching Karate, and working at the restaurant.

"Yeah. Last I checked."

Her face twists. She takes a step back, almost tripping over the two battered suitcases behind her.

"You're—" Her face whitens as she breathlessly regains her balance. "Oh my God. You're a guy."

"And you thought I wasn't?"

"I thought you're a girl. Leslie…" She blows out a sharp breath, shoulders tight. "You know what, never mind."

She's smaller than I expected, pale in the harsh hallway light, with the kind of fragile frame that makes you think she could break under a hard wind. But her hair is a riot of dark curls, wild and stubborn, falling almost to her waist.

And those eyes…wide and unblinking, caught somewhere between fear and fight. They're the kind of eyes you don't forget, even if you try.

I tell myself I'm not looking. I tell myself I'm just being polite, that she's only a roommate, nothing more. But the truth is, something knocks loose in my chest, and I shove it down before it can take shape.

Because I don't do love at first sight. I don't do fragile girls who look like they've lived through more than they should.

And I definitely don't do the way my hands itch to reach out, to steady her.

So instead, I nod, forcing my voice to be calm and neutral.

"Let me guess," I say. "You're Joni Guevarra."

She nods. "This was supposed to be a practical arrangement. When Student Services said someone had a vacancy in their subsidized accommodation, I didn't think twice."

"It can still be practical," I say, trying to keep my voice calm. "I'll stay out of your way."

She mutters something under her breath, then exhales deeply. "Good. I'd like that."

I step aside to let her in.

As soon as she's inside the apartment, I move to the hallway to retrieve her suitcases.

"You don't have to," she says, staring at me again.

"It's okay. I got it."

Without another word—and without looking at her too hard—I bring her suitcases inside and show her to her room.

We make a roommate agreement that night, scribbled in her small, neat handwriting on the back of an old course syllabus:

1. *No visitors after midnight.*
2. *No entering each other's rooms.*
3. *No unnecessary talking.*
4. *No crossing personal lines.*

It's all rules, no warmth. She tapes it to the refrigerator door like some kind of gospel.

I don't argue.

I've lived by a stricter code my entire life.

# CHAPTER 2

## *Not A Dream*

BUT JONI ISN'T EASY TO IGNORE.

She's always up early for work at the university library and the graduate school office. She studies late into the night, books spread across the kitchen table like a fortress. She wears oversized hoodies that swallow her frame, and she chews the ends of her pens until the plastic bends.

And sometimes, I hear her.

Not her studying. Not her muttering over notes.

Her nightmares.

The first time, it's past two in the morning. I'm on the sofa, freshly showered after a long night at the restaurant for my boss' private engagement party, surfing through channels in an attempt to feel sleepy. But I can't fall asleep, a little too happy and excited at the money in the envelope I got as a bonus.

I'm about to message my mother, to tell her I'll be sending her dialysis money earlier that month, when I hear muffled cries bleed through the wall.

It's followed by a choked plea.

*"Stop…please stop."*

I find myself standing outside her door, fist hovering over wood, debating on what I should do.

Rule Number Two says no entering. But rules don't mean much when someone sounds like they're drowning.

I knock softly. "Joni? You okay?"

The sound cuts off.

There's silence, followed a shaky breath.

"I'm fine."

She's not. But I back away.

⌒

Over the weeks, I learn pieces.

Not from her telling me, but from what slips through the cracks.

The way she flinches when a door slams too hard in the hallway.

The way her hands tremble when she hears a man raise his voice, even if it's just people passing outside on the street or an actor on TV.

The way she triple checks the locks on the apartment door before going to bed.

And one night, when the nightmare is worse than usual, I hear her say, *"Don't lock us in, Papa. Please don't."*

My chest burns. I know then.

She didn't just run to grad school for ambition.

She ran to survive.

Despite the rules, we keep colliding.

She makes coffee. I make eggs. She offers me a mug. I offer to make her sunny side-up. We end up eating together in silence.

She hogs the washing machine. I fold her clothes without asking, and she glares but doesn't stop me.

She steals my spare pens. I hide her favorite mug, just to see her scowl.

It's far from a romance. It's not even friendship. It's something raw and jagged in between.

And every time our hands brush—passing a plate, reaching for the fridge handle—something inside me stirs.

Something I'm not supposed to want.

It breaks one night after I come back from the restaurant, still sporting bruised knuckles from sparring earlier that day in preparation for a tournament I'm training the bigger kids in.

She's on the couch, legs curled under her, staring at the blank TV screen.

"You okay?" I ask.

She doesn't answer. Instead, she looks at my hands. "Does it hurt?"

I shrug. "Not really. I'm used to it. Been into Karate since I was four. Teaching since I was eighteen."

She nods. "You had dinner yet? I have some extra *pancit* put aside."

The question makes me freeze midway to my room.

I nod, swallowing hard. "Yeah. Our boss lets us have whatever we want to eat before going home. Saves a lot of money that way, to be honest."

She averts her eyes. "You heard me the other night, didn't you?"

I stare at her. "Heard you?"

Then, in a voice almost too soft for me to hear, she adds, "I used to hear my mother scream when my father hit her. My brother and I were locked in my room. He was younger, so I'd cover his ears. But I heard everything. Every hit."

The air thickens.

I sit down across from her. Not too close, but close enough.

"You're safe now, Joni," I say. "No one's going to hurt you. Not while you're with me."

Her laugh is sharp and bitter. "Safe doesn't stick, Les. It just…slips away."

I want to tell her I'll hold it steady. That I'll fight off every ghost her father ever planted. But I don't.

Instead, I reach over and take her hand. She tenses, but she doesn't pull away.

Her skin is cold. Mine is warm.

Slowly, she lets her fingers curl into mine.

She lifts her eyes, meeting my own. "Has anyone ever told you?"

"Told me what?"

For the first time, I see a smile bloom across her face.

"You look a lot like J-Hope."

# CHAPTER 3

## Not A Rule

THE AGREEMENT BEGINS TO UNRAVEL AFTER THAT. We talk more. We eat together. We sit in silence that isn't empty anymore.

She tells me that her father died from lung cancer last year, and her mother is still teaching at the public elementary school in Kalibo. Her brother is in college at a neighboring district, studying to become a merchant marine. He actually helped her find a job at the university, since the mother of his best friend works at the same place.

I tell her about my father who left us for another woman when I was six, and my mother who used to run a small *manokan* in Bago City before she got too sick to cook. I tell her how Karate got me out of trouble when I was younger, and how I got my first job because of it.

I find out we both want to teach. Maybe abroad.

And one night, after another nightmare, she comes out of her room and knocks on my door at three in the morning. Her eyes are wet, her curls a wild mess.

She doesn't say anything. She just stands there, shaking.

I open my arms.

She steps into them.

The hug is awkward at first, stiff, all edges and hesitation. Then she buries her face against my chest, and I feel her breathe against me, the sound ragged and uneven.

My shirt dampens with her tears. My hand finds the back of her head.

"No one's going to hurt you, Joni," I tell her. "You're safe with me."

She clings tighter.

Then, on my bed, she cries herself to sleep.

From then on, the lines blur.

She tells me she will become too fat because of how well I cook, but eats everything I make for her. I tease her about her caffeine addiction, but she still brings me coffee every single time she makes some for herself.

She sits in the corner of the dojo sometimes while I teach, watching me like she doesn't know if she's impressed or terrified.

She times her trips to Megaworld with my shifts at the restaurant so she's waiting for me when I get off work. One warm summer evening, my boss' fiancée sees her standing outside and admires her curly hair, then invites Joni in for some ice cream, thinking she's my girlfriend. No one admits or denies anything.

We study together, and find out we're both fans of the

Korean action series *The Uncanny Counter*. I tell her the noodle chef lady reminds me of my mother.

And when she dreams bad, she comes to me. Always to me.

The night it all tips over, she's sitting on my bed, knees drawn up, wearing one of my shirts because hers is in the laundry pile. The hem brushes her thighs, and she's chewing her lip like she's daring herself to speak.

"I hate rules," she mutters.

"Then break them." My voice is low, rougher than I mean it to be.

Her head snaps up, eyes wide. Something flickers there—fear, want, maybe defiance—and before I can second-guess it, she leans in and kisses me.

It's clumsy at first, rushed, all teeth and nerves. But the second her lips soften, I ease back, gentling it. My hand cradles the side of her face, fingers brushing her cheek.

She shivers under my touch. "Les…"

"Shhh." I put my arms around her, steadying us both. "We don't have to rush. You call the pace. You tell me what you want."

Her breath hitches, then she kisses me again, firmer and hungrier this time. The sound that escapes her throat is half a whimper, half a demand.

I pull her closer. She fits against me like she's been meant to all along.

"Tell me what to do, Joni," I murmur against her mouth. "It's all about you."

She shakes her head, fingers coaxing the hem of my own shirt upward. "Don't let me go."

And I don't.

I kiss her slowly, deeply, letting her set the rhythm. My hand strokes up her thigh, delving past the fabric of her shorts, careful and tentative at first. When she tilts her hips closer, I take it as permission.

Her breath comes faster, her hands clutching at my clothes, pulling them off with a raw, almost desperate need, until I'm naked.

She helps me undress her, pulling off the borrowed shirt to reveal her bare, perfectly round breasts. Her shorts and panties follow.

I take in the sight of her, feeling dizzy and a little overwhelmed, and draw her close.

"You're safe," I whisper, lips tracing her jaw, her throat. "With me, you're always safe."

Her nails dig into my back as she arches against me, pressing her hips to mine. "Then make me feel it. Tonight. Always."

Something in me breaks loose at those words.

Tenderness changes into heat, the kind that coils low in my stomach. I ease her back onto the mattress, our mouths never parting. She pulls me with her, tugging until my weight settles above her.

The kiss grows fiercer, more desperate, and when she moans into my mouth, I nearly lose it. My hands roam, hers too, until I am rock-hard, until she is warm and soaking wet against me.

Every wall she's built between us crumbles piece by piece, replaced by the way she molds her body against mine, the way she gasps my name, the way she tells me to make her feel everything.

And when we finally cross that last line together, when

she lets me take her and I obey her cries for more, it isn't just about breaking rules anymore.

It's about us rewriting everything.

⁓

The roommate agreement is still taped to the refrigerator door the next morning.

The first four rules are crossed out now.

But at the bottom, in her handwriting, a new line has appeared.

5. *Don't ever let me go.*

And every time I see it, I know I never will.

# A SHADOW HEART

# CHAPTER 1

## The Lights

T HE LIGHTS ARE TOO BRIGHT.

Not the kind I'm used to—neon signs flickering in seedy motels, or the sterile glow of Makati towers. These are cheap, borrowed bulbs strung across bamboo poles, their wires sagging, their glow uneven. But it works. The coffee shop looks alive.

Music spills out into the street, a mix of OPM classics and whatever upbeat trash the DJ they hired could cobble together. The banner above the little shop reads *Brew & Break: Coffee for the Puyat Generation.*

It's all clever. And true.

I know I shouldn't be here, but I am.

The job offer hasn't come in yet. No contract. No instructions.

I'm only here to watch. To learn. That's what I tell myself.

But my eyes keep finding her.

Lara Bienvenides. A politician's daughter. A Congressman's pretty little gem. She shouldn't normally be anywhere near this crowd. The coffee shop is filled with a mix of students in uniforms, call center kids still in ID lanyards, and yuppies clutching cheap plastic tumblers like trophies.

But here she is, with her older brother Luke. He owns the place and she works for him. It's not a secret that they have left their parents to strike out on their own. Their father, Lawrence, had been implicated one too many times in misspent pork barrel investigations and disappearing flood control projects, but he's slipped out all of them fairly unscathed.

Lara has the sleeves of her simple white shirt rolled up. Her hair's tied back, a few strands sticking to her forehead with sweat. She's carrying trays of iced coffee and complimentary cookies, laughing with strangers, brushing errant sugar and crumbs off her jeans as moves around the room.

She looks free.

And it makes something twist in my chest.

A group of young men and women invite me to join their table, but I ignore them. I'm leaning against the far wall, shadowed, my usual place wherever I am. I sip the cold bottle of light beer I bought just to blend in.

My mask is off. Not the cloth one, but the mask of distance. Tonight, I let myself watch.

Later, Luke makes a speech. It's nervous and awkward, about dreams and hard work and no shortcuts. The crowd cheers him on. Lara claps the loudest. Her smile is proud, fond, and real.

It doesn't take long before couples take to the tiny space in the middle of the shop, set up as a makeshift dance floor.

Then the music changes to something slow, almost moody. An old Rivermaya song, maybe.

Before I know what I'm doing, I push off the wall.

Lara's near the counter, wiping away sweat from her forehead with a white handkerchief, a small smile of relief on her delicate face. She looks up, startled, when I stop in front of her.

My voice comes out low and steady. Not a request. Not quite a command.

"Dance with me."

# CHAPTER 2

## The Dance

"**D**ANCE WITH ME."
The words cut through the noise of the crowd. Not loud or demanding. Just steady, like he knew I'd hear him.

I look up, startled, wiping sweat from my forehead with my handkerchief.

He's a stranger, distinctly taller than most people in the room. He's broad-shouldered, hair swept back from his face and tied neatly, face too angular and sharp-featured to be handsome. A scar cuts across his left cheek.

He's dressed too plainly to be one of Kuya's investors, too clean to be one of the neighborhood kids, too casual to be working at one of the offices nearby. It's just a plain black shirt over some dark jeans.

I should laugh, tell him no. But something in his dark eyes holds me still. Something deep and unspoken. I feel like they've been on me all night.

And maybe I like that.

So I nod.

His hand closes around mine. It's large and calloused, his grip warm and certain. My pulse jumps.

He draws me into the open space where couples sway to Rivermaya. His other hand settles at my waist, steady, anchoring me in the crush of the crowd.

My body tenses, then softens as he guides me. He's close, close enough that I can feel the heat of him through my sweaty shirt, close enough that his chest brushes mine when we change tempo or angles.

"What's your name?" I ask, because I need words to distract myself from how hard my heart is beating.

"Jace." His voice is deep, slightly raspy at the edges. I imagine it whispering my name, and heat rushes to my face.

"Jace…" I repeat, trying it out. It fits. Strong, short, and dangerous. "I'm Lara."

"I know." His mouth almost curves, like he's smiling at some private joke.

He doesn't smell like anyone else here—not beer, not sweat, not even cologne. Just rain and smoke and something clean that clings to my skin when I breathe him in.

"You don't look like someone who hangs out at coffee shop launches," I murmur.

"First time." His gaze never leaves mine. "Worth it."

"Well, that's nice to hear," I say. "You should visit more often. Support local businesses."

"Maybe I should," he answers softly. "If I get to see you like this."

I blush again, swallowing as I look away.

He doesn't say anything, but his hand on my waist digs a little deeper into the fabric of my shirt, the heat seeping into my skin underneath.

The song is ending.

I don't want it to.

He leans in, close enough that his breath brushes my ear. "Thank you for the dance. Goodnight, Lara."

And then he's gone.

He just lets me go, as if the moment never mattered, and disappears into the night.

I stand frozen in the middle of the crowd, breathless, my skin tingling where he touched it, my heart still racing like I've just stepped off the rooftop of a skyscraper.

Whatever the hell that was…

I'm not walking away from it unchanged.

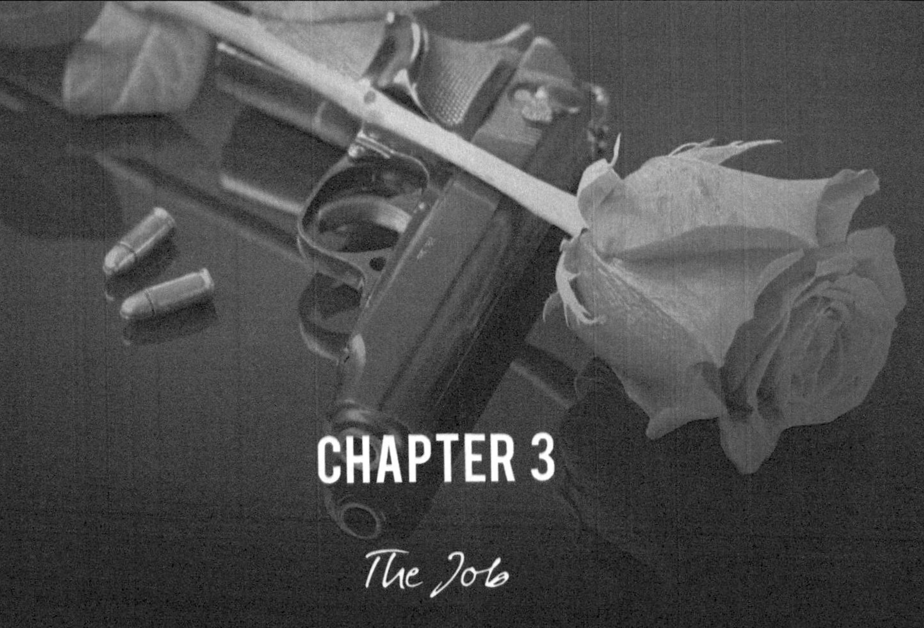

# CHAPTER 3

## The Job

T HE BAR SMELLS OF STALE GIN AND WET ASHTRAYS. I don't remember how many times I've been here before, but I know it's always to pick up my end of a contract. My handler likes the place because no one really asks too many questions.

I sit in the corner booth, shadowed and waiting. The woman arrives late—sharp cream suit, a sharper humorless smile, the kind that says she's paid to make problems vanish. She slides a folder across the table without bothering with pleasantries. This will be my third job with their party.

"Jace," she says, voice smooth. "This one's important. A Congressman's daughter. Leverage. Let's just say we want the old man to get off his high horse."

I don't touch the folder yet. I just listen.

"The girl's visible. Loved by the press. Always on her brother's arm at these little…projects of his. They're trying to build a business empire together, coffee shops and restaurants. A cheap concept, but it makes them accessible, relatable. People like them. Her more so. She's not the usual spoiled rich girl who posts pictures of expensive vacations on social media. She's a college student. All that."

I nod, not saying anything. Politicians don't want their kids to be liked. They want them to be untouchable, just like them. For when the time comes.

"The job is clean," she continues. "Grab her. Hold her. We'll take care of the rest. Price is double your previous fee. We don't want anyone to see or suspect anything. So we got the best in the business for this sort of thing."

I flip the folder open. Photos slide out.

Lara Bienvenides. Up close, in profile, laughing with her brother in front of a coffee cart at Glorietta. Another shot, her in a light dress at some ribbon-cutting event. She looks a bit younger in it.

But it's the same angel of a woman from the party.

Her eyes are just as I remember. Wide, bright, and alive.

I shut the folder before the woman sees too much in my face.

"I'll do it," I say.

"Fifty percent will be wired within the hour," she confirms.

"Make it sixty. I'll let you know when it's time for pick-up." My voice doesn't falter, though my chest feels tight.

She looks at me for a moment, then nods.

"Fine. We'll wait for your call."

༄

In daylight, the coffee shop is small, squeezed between a pawnshop and a convenience store, its new signboard still smelling of paint. Inside, the tables are crowded with students and call center kids nursing cups of cheap caffeine like it's holy water.

I step up to the counter. The menu is handwritten on kraft paper. *Matapang Brew, Puyat Latte, 2AM Americano.*

And then I see her.

She's behind the counter, apron tied around her waist, sleeves rolled up like before. Her thick black hair is in a loose pile at the top of her head. Her skin looks dewy in the soft lights of the shop.

Her brother is in the back arguing with a supplier, and she's running the register herself.

She glances up, and the moment her eyes lock on mine, something clicks into place. Recognition. And wariness. Maybe something else.

For a heartbeat, neither of us speaks.

Then I clear my throat. "Black coffee, please."

She blinks, nods quickly, and turns to pour. The small act—her fingers steady, her hair falling into her face, the steam curling between us—feels louder than the busy chatter of the whole shop.

When she sets the paper cup down between us, our hands almost touch.

"You came back," she says softly.

I wrap my hand around the cup, holding onto the heat. "I said I would. Worth it."

Her lips part, and I see the faintest trace of a smile before she catches herself and looks away.

I turn away without another word, the coffee burning down my throat as I drink it to hide my face.

For the first time in years, the contract feels heavier than the gun under my shirt.

# CHAPTER 4

## *The Walk*

T HE SHOP IS BUSY FOR ANOTHER HOUR OR SO—students bent over their laptops, workers laughing too loudly over greasy plates of fries and sliders, young couples huddled next to each other sharing brownies and carrot cake.

They're the kind of people my brother says we're here for. Affordable coffee and food, decent Wi-Fi, and no one kicking you out if you sit too long.

By the end of my shift, I'm tired. I take off my apron as I say goodbye to the baristas coming in for the night shift. I grab my bag and phone, notebook tucked under my arm for quick reviews during breaks.

I push open the side door, and stop.

He's there.

Jace leans against the lamppost outside the staff entrance, one hand shoved into his jeans pocket, the other loose at his side.

"Hi," I say, a little awkwardly, throat tight. "Waiting for someone?"

"For you," he says simply, as if it explains everything.

I stare at him. "Why?"

"It's late," he says. "I'll walk you wherever you need to go. Or wait until you get a ride."

Something in me wants to argue, to say I can look after myself, to ask what kind of man waits outside a coffee shop for a girl he barely knows. Besides, I know how to handle myself. My father had made sure of that, since Luke and I were kids.

But the truth is, his presence doesn't feel wrong. It feels…protective. Maybe he's already claimed a right to be here, without me knowing.

"I don't need a ride," I tell him as we fall into step together. "I live just a few blocks away. Small apartment. Right next to my brother's. He makes sure I stay in school even with the business. I've got an exam tomorrow."

"You still study?" His gaze flicks to my face curiously.

"Of course I do. Accountancy, actually. I'm not letting Luke carry everything on his back." I hug the notebook tighter to my chest. "He's building something. And I want to be part of it, properly, as a partner in the business. What about you?"

He shrugs. "Computers. A little bit of this and that. Mostly contracts. Never got to finish college, but I get by. I live a few blocks out."

I sneak glances at him. The way the streetlamp hits the sharp lines of his face. The scar half-hidden in the shadows. The way he carries himself—graceful yet quiet, every movement measured.

I can't even tell how old he is. He could easily be twenty-five or forty-five.

Jace doesn't say much as we make our way through the streets, but he doesn't need to. He walks close, his stride steady, like he's watching every shadow we pass.

He's not like anyone I know. He's not like anyone I should ever get close to.

And still, something in me wants to.

We stop at my gate. I should thank him, say goodnight, and go inside.

But instead, I look up at him and the words tumble out on their own. "You didn't have to walk me home."

"I did," he replies, the same way he did earlier.

I don't think.

I put a hand on his shoulder, to make him lean down. Then I rise on my toes and press my lips softly to his. Hesitant but quick, before my courage vanishes.

His breath catches, and I feel the smallest tension in him, as if he might pull me back in for more.

But he doesn't. He lets me have this one reckless choice.

I step away, cheeks hot, heart thundering. "Goodnight, Jace."

I slip inside the building, heart still racing, but I can't quite let it end. The kiss still burns on my lips. The warmth of him still clings to my skin.

So I walk to the small window by my desk and push the curtain aside.

He's still there.

Standing under the lamplight, shoulders squared like he belongs to the night itself. He doesn't move. Then, as if feeling my eyes on him, he looks up straight at my window, and catches me watching.

Heat floods my face and neck. But instead of hiding, I lift my hand and give him a wave.

For a moment, nothing. Then he raises his hand in return. Not playful, not shy—but steady, sure, a silent pact I know but don't understand.

It makes me smile anyway. My chest feels too full, like something new is blooming there, fragile but real.

I lower my hand, letting the curtain fall back into place.

On the street below, I know he's still standing there, still looking.

And I stand in my quiet little room, smiling into the shadows, already falling.

# CHAPTER 5

## *The Night*

I stay until her shift ends.

I listen to the hum of the espresso machine, the sound of chairs scraping against tiles, and the voices of the students and call center kids as they drift out into the night. And still I sit, nursing a coffee gone cold, just to watch her.

Lara moves from table to table, clearing cups and plates. She hums under her breath, absentminded, something soft and tuneless.

She shouldn't be here, in this world where shadows like mine exist. She should belong to the light, where humming and laughter mean something.

Finally, she looks up and sees me still sitting there. Her eyes widen a little. "Jace. You're still here?"

I shrug. "Needed to see how you survived."

Her smile blooms instantly. The sight feels like a full round shot into my chest.

"The exams? Brutal. But I think I passed. Numbers never liked me, but I'm patient with them. Something's gonna give eventually, right?"

"Passing's enough." I lean forward, elbows on the table. "Your brother will be proud."

She tilts her head, studying me like she doesn't quite understand me. "You actually remembered I had exams."

"Of course I did."

Something flickers in her eyes. As if she's not used to people noticing, not like this. She tucks a strand of hair behind her ear, looking flustered, and murmurs, "Most people don't pay attention like that."

I try to smile. As best as I could. "I'm not most people."

She smiles back a little. "No. You're not."

She looks at me for a few more moments before she turns away to finish cleaning up. I watch her pull out her white handkerchief from her pocket and use it to pat away the beads of sweat clinging to her slender neck.

I have never seen something so innocent, yet so erotic. *Fuck it all.*

I should leave. I should end it here. But instead, I wait for her to finish up, then walk beside her into the night.

The streets are quiet, pools of yellow light stretching under the lampposts. A stray dog barks, a tricycle rattles past. When she looks at me, her eyes are tired, but soft, almost gentle.

"You don't have to keep walking me home, Jace. I'm used to this neighborhood."

"I know."

"Then why?"

"Because it's late." I glance at her, voice low. "And I'd rather it be me here than someone else."

She slows, just a fraction, as if the words caught her off guard. "You make it sound like the streets are dangerous."

"They are," I say simply.

She studies me, her eyes trying to see beneath the shadows I wear.

"Not when you're around," she replies.

Silence stretches between us. Every step toward her building feels like another step toward the edge of a cliff I can't stop myself from walking off.

At her gate, she stops, turning to me. The lamplight paints her in gold.

She's nervous. I can see it in the way her fingers tighten on the straps of her bag, in the way her breath catches, but she doesn't look away.

"Jace…" Her voice is barely above a whisper. "You're… very different."

I don't ask what she means. I don't want to hear it.

And then she pulls me down by the shirt and kisses me.

It's soft and tentative at first, but it lingers, her hand brushing lightly against my chest. I feel her heart pounding as fast as mine. When she pulls back, her eyes are shining.

"You're a good man," she says softly.

The words cut through me, raw and merciless. I want to tell her the truth, that I'm anything but, that I'm the danger she doesn't see.

But my voice betrays me. "Don't say that."

"Why not?" she asks gently, almost smiling. "It's true. You look out for me. You don't even realize it, but you do."

Then she reaches up, her fingers lightly tracing over the scar on my cheek.

"You're very special," she says.

I can't breathe.

*She doesn't know.*

Her hand grazes mine as she lowers it and steps back toward her gate. "Goodnight, Jace."

And just like that, she's gone, door closing softly behind her, leaving me outside with my shadows and her words seared into my chest.

*You're a good man. You're very special.*

Just like the night before, I look up to see her standing by the window. She waves to me, a smile on her face.

I wave back.

Then I watch her draw the curtains. I don't move.

I stand there long after the lights in her apartment go dark.

And for the first time in years, I hate myself for the job I already agreed to.

∽

I tell myself not to come.

I tell myself to let her walk home alone tonight, to break the pattern before it becomes something I can't undo.

But I'm here anyway, across the street from where I can see her.

Inside the coffee shop, I see her moving, wiping down a table as she talks to the men coming in for the new shift, stretching her arms like she's already half-asleep.

She's humming again. She doesn't know I hear her through glass, that I carry the sound with me into my dreams.

My chest aches. She waved at me. Smiled at me like I was hers to trust. And today, for hours, I thought about that smile. About her lips pressing to mine at the gate, soft and certain, calling me a good man, telling me I'm someone special.

I almost believed her.

Almost.

Then I remembered the file waiting in my room. Her photo clipped to the top. The promise I made to the woman who pays me to finish this.

And the truth—that nothing about me is good.

The side entrance door opens. Lara steps out, bag slung across her body. She pauses for a moment, glancing down the street.

She's looking for me. I see it in the way her eyes linger on the shadows, the faint crease of disappointment when she thinks I'm not there.

*God.* She wanted me here.

She starts walking. Her footsteps echo against the quiet pavement. I fall into step behind her, silent as I've been trained to be, my body a shadow among shadows.

Three blocks. Then two. My throat is dry.

I should let her go. I should vanish into the dark and forget her name.

I should let the job go.

But my feet move faster.

"Jace?" Her voice is uncertain when I finally step into the spill of the streetlight. She's not afraid. Not yet. She even smiles, faint and relieved. "I thought you weren't coming tonight."

My stomach twists. She doesn't know. She never saw the predator standing in the place of her protector.

I don't answer. I can't. I just reach into my pocket, feel the pouch of dust warm against my palm.

Her smile falters. "What's wrong?"

I step closer. Too close. The scent of coffee and her own cologne clings to her, now dangerously familiar.

"I'm sorry, Lara," I say. "Forgive me."

She opens her mouth to speak, but then I break the pouch, golden powder spilling into the night air.

She gasps, tries to push past me, but her body falters. "Jace…what are you—"

I catch her before she hits the ground. Her head falls against my chest, her lashes fluttering once before the darkness takes her.

I hold her tighter than I should. Too tight for someone who's only a job.

My heart slams against my ribs. She weighs nothing, but carrying her feels like bearing the whole world.

*You're very special.*

Her words echo in my skull.

*You're a good man.*

No. I'm not.

I lift her into my arms and disappear into the waiting shadows.

⌒

The water scalds my skin, but it isn't enough.

I turn the knob hotter, let it burn across my scar, down my chest, over the hands that carried her here. The sting is better than the cold inside me. Better than thinking about the way she said my name before the darkness closed around her.

Steam fills the bathroom, but it doesn't scrub me

clean. The powder dust still clings to my conscience. The lie still rings in my ears.

*You're very special. You're a good man.*

I press my forehead to the tiles and breathe hard. If she knew who hired me, if she knew why, she'd spit at me, claw at me, even fight until she bled.

And yet she smiled at me. She kissed me. She waved from her window.

She believed in a man who never existed.

I twist the knobs off and step out, water trailing down my back, pooling on the tiles. I dry myself quickly, pull on a black shirt and joggers.

No mask now. No gun. Just me. The man in the shadows.

When I open the bathroom door, the room is hushed except for the low hum of the air-conditioner.

She's still asleep.

Lara lies curled on the bed, small beneath the weight of the hotel blanket, her long hair loose and spilled across the pillow. Her breathing is steady, lips parted slightly, face softened into something that feels too pure for the world she's been dragged into.

For a moment, I just stand there. Watching her. Listening to her breathe.

She looks peaceful.

I hate myself for knowing that peace will shatter in a few hours, when I take her to the rooftop. When the client arrives at dawn.

I drag a chair to the far side of the bed, lower myself onto it. My arms rest heavy on my knees, fingers knotting together as if they could hold me in place.

It should be easy. A job's a job. I've done worse.

But I can't stop staring at her. At the girl who called me good. At the girl who kissed me twice, and meant it.

Dawn is coming.

And I don't know if I have the strength to hand her over.

# CHAPTER 6

*The Fall*

Something throbs at the back of my skull, dull and insistent, pulling me up from the dark.

Flashes come back in pieces.

*The street. A scarred face. A voice low in my ear.*

*The sudden blackness.*

I open my eyes.

The room is half-dark, curtains drawn, the ceiling broken by restless shadows. A blanket covers me. The mattress beneath me is soft, molding to my body as though I belong here.

I don't.

My pulse spikes. I push the blanket aside, panic scraping raw against my throat. I'm still in my clothes. The white shirt and denim skirt are both intact, a little rumpled, still smelling faintly of coffee. Nothing has been taken from me but time.

Where am I?

The street. The dust.

Jace.

A trap.

My breath hitches as I force myself upright. My body aches, nerves buzzing from whatever he used.

*I can get through this.*

I see something shift in the corner of the strange room. And I freeze.

He's there, standing at the foot of the bed.

*Jace.*

Even the shadows can't hide him. His dark eyes are unblinking, and the scar cuts a brutal line across his face. His hair falls loose, framing a jaw too sharp, too merciless.

"You." My voice is nothing but a hoarse whisper, but it fills the silence like a scream. "How could you do this? HOW?"

His eyes flicker. Surprise? Regret? I don't know.

My hand closes around the nearest thing I can reach. It's a glass lamp on the bedside table. I yank the plug free.

And before I can think, it's flying through the air.

He moves fast, but not fast enough. The lamp shatters against the wall beside him, shards spraying out like stars. One cuts across his right side. Blood blooms red against his forearm.

He curses low under his breath, clutching the wound.

I don't wait. I run out the nearest exit I can see.

I find myself on the balcony, wrapped in the heavy night air.

Wind slaps at me, whipping my hair across my face. My chest heaves. I glance down. Endless city lights blur into dizzying streams of yellow and red.

It's too far, too high. If I jump, it's to my death.

Behind me, I hear footsteps.

He's coming.

I spin, throwing myself into a stance I've learned from Karate lessons our parents made me take since I was four. My body trembles, but I bare my teeth anyway.

"Get the fuck away from me, you bastard."

He doesn't answer. His eyes are unreadable, his steps deliberate, corralling me like prey.

I strike first. A kick to the midsection, enough to give me space to run past him. But he dodges it. His counter lands, palm to ribs, slamming the air from my lungs.

Pain cracks through me, and I stumble back.

The railing never catches me.

Only air. Only the plunge.

The world is a smear of black and neon and the howl of wind. I scream until my throat tears.

And then…

Impact. Not with the ground, but with him.

An arm locks around my waist, iron and heat. The rope bites above us, our single lifeline as the city spins below.

My scream dies into a gasp.

"Let me go," I choke out, but it's weak, almost pitiful.

"No." His voice is rough and harsh in my ear. "I can't."

I turn my head just enough to see his face.

The mask of shadows is gone. Only his eyes remain, burning and determined.

They're not the eyes of a monster. They're the eyes of a man bleeding.

A drop hits my cheek, warm and metallic.

*Blood.*

His blood. From the arm that holds the rope.

From the wound I gave him.

And still he holds.

We rise, inch by inch, until the railing meets us again. He shoves me over it. My legs shake as they find the solid surface of the balcony.

I want to run. But I don't.

He hauls himself after me, landing in a heap. His shirt is soaked, crimson smearing on his skin, his breath ragged.

We stare at each other, silence heavy as the night. He doesn't move. Doesn't reach for me. Just waits.

I could run. I should.

I kneel in front of him instead. "You're hurt."

His eyes flash in the shadows. "What are you doing?"

My handkerchief is already in my hands, trembling as I press it to his forearm. I knot it tight, clumsy but firm. Blood seeps through anyway. My throat aches. "That will help with the bleeding…for now."

When I look up, he's closer than I expected. Too close. Heat radiates off him, his gaze steady, as steady as the first time I looked into those eyes.

I should hate him. He kidnapped me. He dragged me into this nightmare. But my pulse won't calm, not with his heat seeping into me, not with his eyes dragging me under like tides I can't fight.

His face is inches from mine. His hand brushes my jaw, his thumb grazing my skin like he has every right to. I should recoil. Instead, I shiver.

"Why?" I breathe.

"Because I can't stop," he says. "I can't let go."

Then his mouth claims mine.

The kiss is fire and steel, a clash of everything I should refuse and everything I can't resist. My hands curl into his shirt, pulling him closer, tasting blood and salt and him.

His tongue slides against mine, rough and starving, and I melt into him even as every nerve in me screams danger.

Everything else falls away—the city, the balcony, even the fear. My body betrays me completely, molding against his as though it's been waiting for this.

He drags me onto his lap, his thighs like iron beneath me, his chest hard and hot against mine. The cloth I tied around his forearm is already soaked, blood seeping warm through the fabric, but still his grip is unyielding. One hand digs in my hair, jerking my head back so he can take my mouth deeper, his tongue sliding hungrily against mine.

I moan into him. His other hand finds my hip, then my waist, then lower—gripping, squeezing, dragging me flush against him so I can feel every inch of his arousal pressing against the thin barrier of my skirt.

"Jace," I gasp against his lips, the word breaking.

"You feel that?" he growls, grinding me against him. "You do this to me, Lara. Every single time. That's why."

I shudder, my nails digging into his shoulders, my body rocking helplessly against his. Heat blooms everywhere, consuming and overwhelming.

I should fight. I should pull away. But instead I move with him, straddling him more firmly, my thighs opening over his lap as if my body's already chosen for me.

His hand slips beneath the hem of my skirt, fingers brushing the bare skin of my thigh. I gasp and jolt, but his grip on my hair keeps me right where he wants me.

"Say it," he demands, his breath burning against my mouth. "Say you want this."

"I… I shouldn't…"

"Say it." His fingers skim higher, knuckles grazing the damp fabric of my panties.

A strangled whimper escapes me. "I want you."

He curses harshly, then his mouth is on mine again. His hand presses harder against me through the thin cotton, rubbing slow circles that make my whole body arch into him. My hips grind helplessly against his, chasing the friction, and his groan rumbles through both of us like thunder.

"Goddamn it, Lara," he rasps, biting my lip hard enough to sting. "You'll destroy me."

I'm already destroyed. My body trembles, my thighs shaking as he pushes me closer, closer, until the tension inside me snaps. Pleasure crashes through me, sharp and shattering, and I cry out against his mouth, my release spilling against his fingers.

He holds me through it, murmuring my name, his hand bruising on my hip. And even when the trembling subsides, he doesn't let go. He just pulls me tighter against him, grinding me against his hardness like he can't bear to stop.

I lean close, lips brushing his ear. "Let me give you this too."

His eyes widen, before he growls something low in his throat. His grip loosens just enough for me to slide down, my hand trailing over his chest, his abdomen, until I reach the hardness straining in his pants.

He hisses through his teeth as I palm him firmly, feeling the weight of him hot and pulsing in my hand. His head falls back against the railing, his jaw clenched, a raw sound tearing out of him.

"Lara…"

I stroke him through the fabric, slow at first, then harder, faster, watching him come apart under me. He grabs my wrist like he wants to stop me, but he doesn't. He can't. He's panting now, hips jerking into my hand, his body trembling with need.

I draw closer, mounting him until my hips are just above his thighs. Enough for him to feel that whatever he's feeling, I'm feeling it too.

"Let go, Jace," I whisper into the night. "Let go."

He swears, a guttural sound, before crushing his mouth to mine again. His kiss is frantic, teeth and tongue and desperation, even as his release builds under my hand. When I finally reach inside his waistband and wrap my fingers around him, hot and rigid and slick with need, he shudders violently.

"Fuck…" he groans against my mouth, thrusting into my fist, every muscle in his body drawn tight. I stroke him harder and harder, faster and faster, my other hand tangled in his hair, until he breaks.

His release spills hot across my hand, across his skin, and he buries his face in my neck with a hoarse cry, clutching me like I'm the only thing keeping him alive.

For a moment, it feels like I am.

When his breathing finally slows, when the tremors ease, he cups my face in his hand. I can feel the rope burns on his palm. His eyes are molten, tortured, and tender all at once. He kisses me softly this time, a contrast so sharp it hurts.

And I know…we are not done.

Not even close.

I know what he wants. I know what *I* want.

For one wild, terrifying second, I want him to take me

right here, on the balcony, under the stars with the city lights watching.

I'm still shaking when he kisses me again, his chest heaving. His hands are trembling as they find my cheeks, blood from his wound slick and sticky against my skin.

"I don't want to run," I say against his mouth.

"If I keep you," he rasps brokenly, fiercely, "I destroy you."

The words should terrify me. Instead, they break me open.

Because even as he says it, he goes hard beneath me, throbbing against the soaked cotton of my panties, his body trembling with the effort to hold back.

I can't let him.

I kiss the corner of his mouth, tasting salt and blood and pain.

And I say the words.

"Then destroy me."

# CHAPTER 7

## The Dawn

SOMETHING INSIDE ME SNAPS.

I drag her against the cold concrete of the balcony, my hands rough, my body trembling with the kind of hunger I've buried since the moment I laid eyes on her.

The city is a blur below us, nothing but lights and noise. Here, it's only her. Her breath shudders into my mouth as I claim her lips, as if she's always been mine. I yank her skirt up, my hand pulling down the thin scrap of her soaked panties.

I stop for a moment. Not out of mercy, but because I feel her trembling, not just from fear.

I slide my fingers over her heat, testing and coaxing.

She's wet.

She's wet *for me*.

The realization nearly undoes me. So I do the only thing I could.

I lift her leg, nearly tearing her skirt in half, and bury my mouth in her. She tastes like cream, sweet and a little sticky, as my tongue lap at the juices from her earlier climax.

"Jace," she gasps, pulling at my hair with both hands, her hips jerking closer to my face.

I don't answer. Using my uninjured arm, I reach for her breasts under the cover of her shirt and bra, fingers stroking the nipples as my lips devour the soaking spot between her legs.

"I know, baby," I say against her thigh. "I know. You're ready for me."

"Jace," she says again, her knees bending over my shoulders as she writhes beneath me.

I slide up, covering her body with mine. It doesn't take long for me to lower the joggers, to free myself from the briefs completely. She moans as she pulls my shirt off, her teeth dragging across the bare skin of my chest, her hands digging into my arms, drawing more blood from the wound she'd given me.

And I'm above her, a breath away from making her completely mine.

"Tell me no, Lara," I rasp against her throat, my teeth scraping her skin. "I'll let you go. I promise."

One word could save her.

One word would save me.

"I won't," she says against my lips, then she drags her mouth to my scar, her tongue flicking out to trace it. "Never."

That single word breaks me. I push inside her, and the world explodes.

She gasps, her body so tight. Too tight.

My chest seizes when I realize.

She's untouched. Pure. I'm the first.

"Lara," I groan, my lips finding hers again. "God, you'll break me."

Her nails dig into my back, and I groan louder, half in agony, half in need. I can't stop. I move inside her, slow at first, then harder, deeper, claiming her in every way I know how.

She arches into me, tears glinting at the corners of her eyes, pain and pleasure tangled together.

"You'll destroy me, baby," I growl, kissing her hard, my hips driving her against the concrete until I feel it almost crack.

"Oh, god…Jace!" Her voice breaks on my name. "Don't stop. Please, don't stop—"

Her plea undoes whatever control I had left. I take her brutally, but my hand cradles her face, my mouth drinks every cry she makes. I move faster and faster, until I feel her clench around me, her scream muffled against my lips.

I spill into her with a ragged, broken cry, every drop of me claiming her. I clutch her as if letting go means death.

For one blistering moment, we're one. Flesh and soul and shadow.

When it ends, I collapse against her, our sweat and my blood between us.

Her scent clings to me. Her heartbeat thunders against my chest, wild and alive. And in that moment, I know the truth I've fought to deny since the beginning.

I love her.

God help me, I love her.

"I should never have touched you," I say, pressing my lips to her soaked hair.

Her hand cups my jaw, her eyes steady despite what I've made of her. "But you did. And I'll never regret it."

I kiss her once more. It's soft and reverent, because it's

the last time I'll ever be allowed to. Then I pull away, the shadows closing back around me like a noose.

"Your bag's in the closet. Take my jacket if you want to."

She stares at me. "What are you talking about?"

I don't answer at first. Even as I stand before her bleeding, heart torn open, I help her back into her clothes. I put my arms around her waist and pull her up. I press my lips to her forehead, running my hand through her hair.

I know. I'll never get to touch her like this again.

"Run, Lara," I say softly. "This is the last mercy I have left."

She doesn't move.

"Jace…"

I turn away. "I promised I'll let you go."

Then I walk into the room and sit on the same chair at the foot of the bed.

She stumbles in after me, still wobbly on her feet. It doesn't take long for her to find her things. She slides my jacket on, the fabric swallowing her smaller frame.

She looks at me for the last time, reaching for the doorknob.

"I don't know what to say," she says, her voice small.

I smile at her. "You never had to say anything. Goodbye, Lara."

She doesn't answer.

In a breath, she's gone. Her hair loose, her skirt torn, my blood still drying on her skin.

I watch her from the balcony.

She reaches the street without incident, and mercifully manages to hail a taxi.

I should feel empty. Instead, I feel alive for the first time in years.

"Lara," I whisper into the night, her name torn out of me like prayer.

Like damnation.

I could chase her. I could take her back. I could burn the world down and keep her. I could wage war and win against impossible odds.

I could do it all for her.

But I don't.

Because if I love her at all, I have to let her go.

So I sink into the shadows again, bloodied and haunted, with nothing left but the taste of her on my lips and the fire she's branded into my heart.

And I wait for dawn to come.

# THE HOTEL ROOM

# CHAPTER 1

*The Twilight*

**T**HERE HE IS.

I don't expect him to be there when I open the door.

But he proves me wrong.

I don't ask why he chooses to meet in the same hotel I do. Maybe it's coincidence. Maybe it's fate, or maybe fate is just another word for good timing but with all the wrong reasons.

He leans against the doorframe as if he belongs to the twilight, all shadows and half-hooded eyelids. He smells like cigarette smoke, wearing the same dark blue jacket from years ago.

He doesn't look at me right away.

And I remember the first time I saw him, all those years ago. I was his supervisor at the insurance company and he'd been an encoder. He'd been the fastest to meet quotas in my team, but he never said much to anyone. After a month, he started waiting for me to finish work, then waited until I got into my taxi. He even asked me to text him once I reached home.

Months later, he got into the taxi with me. I took him to a motel.

Then I moved to a government office in Manila.

"You're late," I tell him.

"You aren't supposed to be here," he replies, finally meeting my eyes. "What will they say about their golden girl sneaking around?"

I shake my head, a little tiredly. "And yet here we are."

"Here we are," he echoes, giving me a smile.

It's lopsided, weary, familiar. God, it's familiar.

It's always like this with us. Half-smiles. Half-truths. Half-promises. All of them crumbling at the edges.

The door clicks shut behind him. The rain outside is a distant hush against the windowpane. He shrugs off his damp jacket, tosses it onto the armchair like he owns the room, like he owns this silence between us. But he doesn't. He never did.

The room is quiet except for the hum of the city below. Floor-to-ceiling windows show a skyline we both once dreamed of conquering.

"This is a big change," he says softly, leaning against the wall, watching me, his eyes tracing every movement like he hasn't forgotten a thing. "The room's clean, for a start. Surprised you said you're going to foot the bill. My baby girl can afford better now, can't she?"

I scowl at him. I got the room at a discount using the Undersecretary's name, but I don't want to give him the satisfaction of being right.

"Don't call me that," I bite out instead. "I'm not your baby. And I'm definitely not a girl."

He frowns down at me. "You'll always be to me, Lee."

I shake my head, then sit at the table and pour a glass of red wine.

"Fancy," he murmurs.

I incline my head in casual agreement, as if I didn't book this hotel because of him. As if we didn't always end up together, somehow, when the world got too complicated and we ran out of excuses not to forget.

At least for a while.

He doesn't ask for a drink, but I pour for him too. Old habits, I guess.

We used to drink light beer and eat fried chicken, after the motel.

"I thought you would appreciate something…different," I say.

He smiles.

But I know he doesn't do different. He'd self-destructed weeks after I left my old workplace. By the time I'd heard about it from practically everyone at the insurance company, I was already far away from Iloilo.

"How long are you gonna be in town for?" he asks, sliding into the seat across mine. The soft light of the room cast half his face in eerie, distorted shadow.

"Just the night," I answer. "I'm flying back to work tomorrow evening. I told my boss I'm visiting my parents."

He lifts his glass to me in a mock toast. "Clever girl."

I don't answer, choosing instead to let the word go. I take a sip of my wine, not looking at him but at the bed before us.

"So why now?" he asks softly. "Why this room, this night?"

I sigh. "I know what happened. What you did when I left. You shouldn't have done that."

"What did I do?" he challenges me, almost immediately.

"You didn't listen to anyone. You completely and utterly disregarded all authority by nearly killing Doc Simeon. You're lucky they didn't have you arrested."

He slams the glass down, wine sloshing all over the polished wood. Then he jumps to his feet.

"I didn't come here for this bullshit," he says. "I came for you."

In the dim light, I can see his shoulders shaking, but his voice sounds steady.

"I know," I answer softly.

I put my own glass down and stand, blocking his way.

"That's why I'm here. I want to ask you to stop whatever it is you're doing before you can't anymore."

He shakes his head. "I can't, Lee. You know I can't."

"Dennis." His name escapes my lips, an apology he never asked for. An apology I could never say out loud.

He winces at the sound—and there it is.

That knife-twist in my chest. The one I thought I'd buried under logic and time.

The familiar, breathless tightness whenever I look into his deep-set eyes, so dark they're almost black.

I miss him.

"I love you, Lee," he says. "I loved you the moment you told the VP you could put me to work. You never judged. You just believed."

The pain reaches my stomach, making me feel deathly cold.

*Love.*

He still loves me.

But I don't say it back.

"I still believe," I say cautiously. "And I never judged you. I knew you were better than everyone else, even if you didn't finish college. I never looked at what you had on paper."

He freezes, his body wound tight like a rubber band ready to snap.

"I looked at you," I continue. "I still see you. I still see the man who promised me he won't let me down."

"I promised *you*," he retorts icily. "I didn't promise any of them. When Simeon questioned my work, I told him to fuck off and retire. He shouted at me, made everyone hear that I was a dropout who couldn't even meet quota. So I broke his nose. People forget I used to be good at Silat."

I sigh impatiently. "Christ."

"It was never the same without you, baby girl," he says, softer now. "It all got fucked up so quickly. I didn't even realize I was already fired. I was just too…mad."

"At me," I offer.

He shakes his head. "No. At the world. At them. Never at you."

That does it.

I put my arms around him. His heartbeat thunders in my ear.

"Don't go then," I say. "Stay. Stay the night."

"Say it then," he mutters into my hair. "Just say it, Lee."

I take a deep breath.

"I love you, Dennis." And I just couldn't stop there. "I miss you. It's not the same without you."

He doesn't answer right away. He doesn't even move an inch.

"You should have just told me the minute I walked through that door," he finally says. His eyes take me in, up and down, lips to throat, chest to forehead.

I shake my head and step back, but he reaches for me, hands sliding around my waist.

"I wanted to make sure you're still not completely insane," I shoot back. "I heard stories. Not so flattering ones, I'm afraid."

He laughs then. That low, familiar sound that vibrates through me like a memory I could never shake.

I sit on the edge of the bed. He joins me a beat later.

We're not touching, but the space between us is electric.

"So," I say, "do you want to talk about it?"

He doesn't say anything in response. He just looks at me like he's memorizing every inch of me all over again. I can see it in his eyes.

"Do you remember the first time?" he asks instead.

"The motel in Molo? Or us?"

"Both."

I close my eyes. I remember the rain. I stayed back at the office to sign hundreds of new membership cards. I remember the feel of his hand around mine as he slid into the taxi next to me.

The way he asked me, "Do you want to forget everything for a while?"

It felt like a lifetime ago.

"You made me feel like flying," I say, smiling a bit.

Now, he touches my hand, lightly. "You said you didn't believe in forever. You said you believe in seizing the moment."

"And you said you didn't believe in anything at all."

We both lie sometimes.

He doesn't answer. Not with words.

He moves closer. His hands slide into my hair, and mine find his chest.

"Tell me to stop, Lee," he breathes.

"I can't."

And I don't.

The clothes come off in pieces, peeling away the years between us. Our touches feel like confessions we could never say.

It's like no time has passed at all. His hands know the slope of my hips. My mouth remembers the taste of his name. We fall back into each other like drowning people finding air.

The night is slow, lingering, beautiful. We spend it tangled in the thick white sheets. Fingers skimming skin. Kisses that ask questions, ones answered only in gasps and caresses.

When he whispers my name, tells me he missed *us*, I wonder if he feels it too—the pain of something lost and almost found again.

We don't promise anything.

But we say *I love you.*

Because in this hotel room, that is the most real thing in the world.

# CHAPTER 2

## The Mark

**W**E DON'T SLEEP.

Morning comes quietly. The light is gentle as it skims over my skin, filtering in small ripples through the blinds.

He holds me close and says, "This doesn't change anything."

"I know," I answer. "At least I tried."

But we both feel it. That thing in the air. That almost that always threatens to become more, if only we let it.

He kisses me squarely on the mouth.

"I think that's why I love you," he murmurs against my lips. "And that's why you'll leave."

A lone tear slides down my cheek. He brushes it away with the back of his hand, exhaling softly.

"Promise me you'll do better," I tell him. "Just try. Not for me. For you. You deserve more than what you're doing to yourself."

He pulls me closer, his fingers running through my hair.

"I already had more," he says. "I had you."

The dam finally breaks.

I spend the sunrise crying in his arms.

He doesn't say anything. He just keeps holding me, soothing my tears with soft kisses and feather-light touches.

The last thing I remember is seeing his skinned knuckles, his callused palms, as his fingers trace the gentlest lines down my cheeks.

"Goodbye, Dennis," I say softly, dreamily, before drifting off to an exhausted sleep.

℘

The room is bright when I wake up.

I check the time on my phone, then stare at the ceiling. I know before I look around the room.

He's gone.

A note sits on the nightstand in his handwriting.

Still blocky, a little too sharp. Just like him.

*Thank you for the night. You'll always be my baby girl.*

I trace the words, the same way I traced the hard, sullen lines of his face.

And in the quiet between heartbeats, in the space where the tears and the ache should be, I realize something.

We never made promises.

But love doesn't need those to leave a mark.

It just needs one night.

# THE GIRL WITH THE ALMOND EYES

# CHAPTER 1

## The Green Umbrella

I WAS FOURTEEN THE FIRST TIME I SAW HER.

She was standing beneath the awning outside our school's administration building, holding a green umbrella speckled with cartoon frogs. Her uniform was soaked at the hem, her shoes ruined by the heavy rain, but she looked like summer anyway.

She had long black hair, wind-kissed cheeks, and a smile like sunlight breaking through clouds.

She smiled at me, almost gently. Her almond eyes took in the soaked version of me like someone who actually mattered.

"You look like you need this," she said, offering me her umbrella, moving over to make room for me.

I didn't take it.

Instead, I memorized the shape of her fingers on the curved plastic handle, the way her wet hair clung to her cheek, the rhythm of her voice.

I wrote about her that night.

It was a poem, I realized later on. My first one.

She never knew.

Her name was Mireya.

She lived in a small white house with potted daisies on the windowsill, while I lived two blocks over, in a place that never smelled like anything but old rust and rain that never dries.

People called me Niko.

The boy with the busted life and even more busted shoes. My father was in prison. My mother didn't come home unless she had to; she lived in bingo halls and at mahjong tables instead.

I saw her every day in school. She liked to sit beneath the fire escape behind the cafeteria and read. Sometimes I pretended to smoke just so I could sit near her. She'd wrinkle her nose and say, "That'll kill you, you know."

I shrugged. "So will living."

She never laughed at that. She'd just glance at me with those almond eyes and say, "Don't make dying your ambition."

I didn't know how to tell her it already was.

I watched her from the corners of hallways, the back of classrooms I snuck into just to see her.

She always noticed people, even the invisible ones. She talked to me sometimes. She once gave me a stick of banana cue when I had nothing to eat. She even laughed at a joke I didn't mean to say out loud.

She was kind. Unshakably, stupidly kind.

Mireya didn't belong in my world.

But she lived in my poetry.

I started writing because of her. I hid my poems in notebooks and later, when I joined the gang, in scraps of receipt paper and cigarette boxes.

I never gave her one. I never had the guts. But I wrote like I was bleeding ink. Like every line might save me.

When we were seventeen, she gave me a Band-Aid. I had a broken lip and a bruised eye from a fight I didn't win, and she pressed it into my hand like it was a treasure.

"You don't have to keep doing this, Niko," she said.

But I did. For my brothers who were my only real family. For the streets of De la Rama. For the ones who would die if I didn't hold the line.

Life caught up with me, as it always does.

My father died in a riot at the provincial jail. My mother's lungs gave up on her and the cigarettes she loved more than me.

I didn't go to college. I joined the Marilas, made it a full-time job. Not because I wanted to. Because I had to. We were the ones who kept order at the docks. We were monsters, but we were family.

And still I wrote.

In ink and shadows, in blood and silence. I wrote her name in letters I never sent. Wrote apologies I could never give. Wrote confessions I never had the courage to say.

Wrote about another life, one where I could actually

stand under the frog umbrella with the almond-eyed girl of my dreams.

She stayed in the city and became a nurse.

She always helped out in our neighborhood, smiling at those who came in pain, in need, and in desperation. Once, I saw her patch up a teenaged boy who got shot in a turf fight. No questions asked, even when she saw our colors.

She looked at me then.

"Niko," she said. "You look tired. Do you need anything?"

She spoke without fear. Without judgment.

I couldn't even answer.

I left before I did something stupid.

We crossed paths again and again. At the public market. A church pew. A wake for someone we both knew. She always said hi. I always froze.

My brothers laughed and said she was too good for me. I agreed.

But I wrote her another poem.

# CHAPTER 2

## The Black Coffee

ONE NIGHT, I SAW HER IN AN ALL-HOURS COFFEE SHOP near the river. She wore her hair in a braid, and her white uniform was rumpled from what must have been a long shift.

I asked for two black coffees from the counter. I didn't realize my own hands were trembling as the barista handed me the change.

I went to the tiny two-seat table she had settled on outdoors.

"May I join you?" I asked as I put one of the red cardboard cups in front of her.

She looked up, not surprised at all to see me. She only nodded.

Her almond eyes took me in closely as I settled on the stool across hers.

"You look…" she began, but trailed off.

I waited.

"You still look tired, Niko."

I gave her a smile that didn't reach anything. "You remembered me. And my name."

"I remember everything."

I wanted to say it then, more than anything.

*Then why didn't you see I was always yours?*

But I didn't.

I finished my coffee without saying another word, but I left something on the table, in the space between our red cups.

It's one of my old poems written on the inside of a cigarette box.

She didn't say anything.

I didn't look back.

❦

The war came fast.

Turf was turf. Blood was blood. De la Rama was ours, even if the Valientes didn't agree.

We lost three boys in one week.

I told myself I was doing it for the family. But in my darkest moments, when I stood in the rain with my hands still shaking from the blade or the gun or the weight of the choice, I thought of her.

The girl with the almond eyes who once told me to live.

I didn't expect the bullet. No one ever does.

It tore through my side like fire.

I bled out in the alley behind the videoke bar, beneath a flickering light and the eyes of the patron saint of voyages painted on the dock walls.

My phone buzzed once. It was a message I'd scheduled to send at nine in the evening.

To her.

Somehow, I knew tonight was going to be it.

The message just had three lines:

*You were my sun.*

*You were the only thing that made me write.*

*I hope you smile when you think of me.*

I closed my eyes thinking of her hands. Of the Band-Aid and the banana cue.

Of the green umbrella with the frogs.

Of the moments she always said my name like it meant something more than just a boy life threw to the wind without a second thought.

I thought of her first words to me.

*"You look like you need this."*

This time, I answered. Because I knew this was my last chance.

*Yes, Mireya. I need you.*

*I love you. I always will.*

Maybe, in another life, I would have joined her under the umbrella, in the space she made for me.

Maybe, then, I would have made her mine.

But in this one…

She was the only poem I ever finished.

# CHAPTER 3

## The Red Bag

H E DIES ON A THURSDAY.

I didn't understand the message I got from him that night, but I do now.

I find out on a Saturday, when a man with eyes like steel and tattoos like maps knocks on our gate at almost midnight.

He's terrifying, tall and built like a tank, wearing a nondescript black shirt and faded camouflage pants. He doesn't speak at first. He just stares at me.

Then he hands me a red reusable bag. As I take it with trembling hands, I hear pieces of paper and cardboard scrunching against each other.

"I'm Mart Marila," he says at last. "Niko's brother."

I nod, swallowing hard, too afraid to blink.

"He wrote these for you," he says, voice low, like it hurts to speak. He tilts his head at the bag. "We found them with his things."

He doesn't stay. He nods once and disappears into the night like a shadow.

I lock up and go inside the house. I sit on the sofa and pour out the bag's contents onto the low table.

Inside are poems. Dozens of them, maybe even more than a hundred. All scribbled onto torn cardboard packaging or oddly shaped sheets of paper.

Some of them are half-finished, some torn, all bleeding with longing. My name is in every one.

So is the name of the boy with the bruised knuckles and tired, sad eyes. The boy I always noticed. The boy I always wanted to save.

The boy I wanted to give my heart to, but never let me in.

I sit and read until the sun comes up.

I cry like I never cried before.

And when I finish the last one, I kiss the piece of cardboard, the one where Niko had doodled a girl with an umbrella surrounded by frogs and hearts.

I kiss the words he had written in red ink.

You were my first warmth.
You were the only good thing I never touched, the
    dream I never deserved, the sun I watched rise
    from a rooftop, knowing I would always belong
    to the night.
I wrote you poems you'll never read.
You smiled at me like I wasn't lost.
You looked at me like I mattered.
I think that's what saved me for as long as it did.
And I'm sorry.
I'm sorry I couldn't be better. Sorry I never told you.
I wish I could see you one last time. I wish you could
    read this. I wish you could have known.

I loved you.
I loved you more than any of them will ever
   understand.
I hope you never forget to carry your umbrella.
It's raining again.
And I remember everything about you.

~ Niko


And I whisper into the bleeding dawn, "I remember everything, too, Niko."

# FLOWERS FOR THE DEAD

# CHAPTER 1

## The Daisy and the Lily

I DON'T KNOW HIS NAME.

But every time I pass the plaza near the old church, he's there. Always kneeling in the soil, sleeves rolled up, arms flecked with dirt, hands cradling blooms like they're made of glass. He moves like sunlight, warm and unhurried.

And whenever he sees me, he smiles.

*That* smile.

I'm supposed to avoid patterns. Routine breeds vulnerability. But I can't stop walking by the plaza since I moved to Arevalo.

Not when I know he'll be there. Not when I know, without fail, he'll leave a flower on the edge of the bench I always pass.

Today, it's a yellow-orange daisy. Bold and bright, almost defiant, against the cloudy day around me.

I pick it up, twirl the stem between my fingers, and keep walking.

I'm a killer.

It's what I do. What I was made for.

The men who raised me never gave me real names. Just contracts and an unbreakable professional code.

To them, I was never even a girl. Or a woman.

I'm just Max.

They carved instinct into my spine, turned emotion into static, and told me love was weakness. I believed them for years.

Then came him.

I don't know why I started watching him. Maybe it was the way he treated every flower like a miracle. Or the way he hummed to himself, off-key and soft.

No mask. No pretenses. Just…peace.

I don't know peace. I know orders, targets, and a hundred ways to make each kill look different from the others.

Still, I make time to pass by.

I reroute. I learn he comes every morning by six. I learn he doesn't use gloves because he says the flowers feel sadness when they're touched by something artificial.

One morning, he catches me watching.

"You always look so sad," he says. The gentleness in his voice hits me like a bullet.

I don't answer. I can't.

He kneels down and pulls a lily from a pallet. "This one's for you. It's for healing."

I stare at the glistening white petals. I don't take it.

He places it on the ground next to my feet before turning back to his work.

For the first time, I don't pick up the flower he gave me.

# CHAPTER 2

## The Bullet and the Blood

**M**Y LATEST TARGET IS SOMEONE IMPORTANT.

Big businessman with lots of guards. The client is a politician who knows the businessman plans to run for the Congress spot of his district.

The job takes weeks to plan.

And when it goes wrong—when I underestimate their firepower, when the sirens come faster than I expected—I run.

I'm bleeding. My left side burns where the bullet grazed me.

There's nowhere to go. No safehouse close. No contact who won't ask questions.

Except him.

I stumble into the plaza, lungs screaming.

The sun is just rising, casting gold over everything.

And he's there.

He sees me right away. I hear the muffled sound of his spade hitting the dirt.

He rushes to my side, but couldn't reach me on time.

I collapse at his feet.

"Help," I rasp. "Please."

He doesn't ask any questions. He doesn't even say anything. He just lifts me in his arms and carries me to the sidecar of his *pedicab*.

I hear him breathe a little heavier as he pedals away from the plaza.

His house smells like rosemary and soil. There are pots of aloe vera by the window and a bundle of roses on the table. He lays me on his sofa, working silently and efficiently.

He cleans the wound with surprising ease.

As he stitches me up, he says softly, "I'm Ronnie."

"Max," I answer.

Then I pass out.

⸙

When I wake, it's night.

He's sitting across from me, reading. When I move, he looks up.

There's no fear or anger or wariness on his face. Just… concern.

"You're lucky," he says. "That bullet could have ended you."

I try to sit up. Pain sears through me. "You should have left me."

He shrugs. "Didn't want to."

"You don't know me."

"I know enough. You're tired. You're alone and sad. And you're not as bad as you think."

He hands me a steaming cup of coffee.

"You could have gotten into trouble," I tell him.

He smiles. "But I didn't."

I stay. I don't mean to, but I do.

A week passes, then two. I sleep on his couch. I start helping him water the plants. He teaches me their names.

I find out he wanted to be a doctor and was even studying in college to be one. He'd dropped out on his third year to look after his sick mother, who ran a small flower garden that had been in her family for generations. His father, who died while he was still in high school, had worked for the church and the convent, doing maintenance and gardening. When his mother passed away five years ago, he simply took on the jobs they left behind.

One night, as I warily look at the rice cooking in the silver pot, I ask, "Why do you keep giving me flowers?"

He gives me a thoughtful look as he unwraps a small parcel of *liempo* he'd bought from the market. He now knows it's my favorite.

"Because you look like someone who's never been given anything just because," he answers, the words spoken a little too slowly and honestly for my liking.

I could only stare at him.

"And I like seeing your eyes soften," he adds. "You're beautiful, but the first time I gave you that pink rose, your eyes glowed like sunrise. Maybe that's why. You remind me of the light during sunrise."

We don't kiss until the night before I'm supposed to leave.

I haven't told him. I can't. I don't know what this is, what I'm allowed to feel.

But I break when he brushes a soil-stained hand on my cheek and whispers, "You don't have to go, Max."

So I kiss him.

It feels like everything I never let myself want.

That night, we don't sleep.

That night, I let myself believe.

That I could want something, and be wanted back.

# CHAPTER 3

## The Past and the Sun

BUT I KNOW—THE WORLD ISN'T SOFT. It's a harsh, judgmental bastard, just like the men who created me.

My past catches up.

They find me in my safehouse near the mangrove reserve.

They tell me to finish the contract. One last target. One last loose end.

After this, they promise me I could leave. Or live. Depends on who says what, really.

I tell them to stuff the money up their asses. I tell them we're quits once the job is done.

But that night, I bleed again.

This time, it's so much worse.

But I remember the light in his eyes, the stains on his hands, the warmth of his lips.

So I go back to the plaza at sunrise.

One last time

I collapse on the bench where he left me flowers.

I can't breathe. Everything hurts.

I close my eyes.

Then…

I feel him.

Arms lifting me.

His voice sounds distant, panicked. "No. No, no, no. You don't get to leave me now."

I try to smile. "You're here. You're finally here."

He cries.

As the world begins to turn black, I say the words. "Thanks, Ronnie. Love you."

∽

I wake to sun through linen curtains.

To the smell of roses and lilies on the table.

My body hurts, but I'm alive.

He's asleep beside the sofa, bundled in a thin blanket on a mat on the floor next to me. There's dried dirt on the hem of his pants and dark circles under his eyes.

I reach for his soil-stained hand.

"Ronnie?"

He stirs.

His eyes flutter open, then a smile spreads across his face.

"You stayed," I say.

"I told you," he answers. "You're not alone."

He stands up and takes something from the table.

He sinks to his knees before me, and hands me a bright, bold, and defiant daisy.

"I don't think I want to be alone anymore," I tell him.
He nods, then kisses me.
I kiss him back.
"Then you'll never be," he murmurs against my lips.
And for the first time, I believe I'm allowed to stay.

# MIST
# AND
# BLOOD

# CHAPTER 1

## The Dojo

**T**HE GRAY BUILDING APPEARS AT THE EDGE OF THE shore.

The mist parts, and I see what they call 'the dojo.'

There's no sign, no path.

There is nothing to attract or welcome students.

The place just…exists.

I first heard about it from an old woman who sold me Indian mangoes at the market. She took one glance at the bruise on my cheek and told me to find "the house where the Master lives."

Apparently, he'll teach me to dish it out just as well as I take it.

The other people at the market say the house has always been here, crouched like a waiting beast between the wet trees and the rocks that cradle the sea.

You don't find it on maps. You don't stumble into it by accident. You arrive when you have nowhere else to go.

I arrive on a Monday.

At least, I think it's Monday, because I'm wearing my school uniform.

My shoes are almost ripped in half. My lip is split from a fight I didn't win. My breath comes shallow, most likely from a bruised rib. My stomach's hollow, but my eyes burn. My wrists are a map of old bruises—some that faded into memory, others still pulsing beneath the skin.

I walk through the early morning fog, my arms wrapped around myself—not for warmth, but for armor. The plain gray walls rise out of the mist like something ancient. The roof is heavy with leaves. The courtyard pools with rain.

And the Master is there.

I don't know his name.

He looks like stone carved into a man—angular face, high cheekbones, narrow jaw, eyes that look like the mist I just walked through. His hair is long and black streaked with silver, tied back like a warrior from a forgotten time.

He watches me. I don't know if he's being kind or cruel or curious.

He's just still.

He even doesn't ask why I'm here.

He just picks up my soiled green backpack full of torn clothes and walks into the dojo.

And I follow.

# CHAPTER 2

I LEARN AND SERVE IN SILENCE.

No formal greetings. No initiations. Just days that become weeks that become months.

I don't go to school, but I read the books that fill the shelves in the hallway.

I cook and clean and do laundry. I go to the market in town. He gives me money to buy supplies and pay bills.

I talk to the students and their parents like a model employee.

I sleep in a tiny outhouse at the edge of the property, nestled between groves of coconut trees.

The rest of the time I don't stop training.

He never raises his voice. He doesn't praise or scold.

He exists like gravity. Something I adjust to, something I resist. Something I eventually learn to trust.

When I stumble, he catches me.

When I scream, he lets me.

When I collapse, he waits.

When I get the attacks in the middle of the night, he

carries me to the dojo and lets me cry myself to sleep on the mats.

I learn to move with precision. To strike without hesitation. To still my breath until even the rain sounds like rhythm. My fists learn to break brick. My muscles harden. My fire refines itself, no longer wild, but contained and ready.

And at night in my tiny outhouse, my heart racing with echoes of old horrors, I feel him there.

Something near enough to reach.

# CHAPTER 3

*The Typhoon*

**T**HE YEAR'S TYPHOON SEASON IS THE MOST CRUEL YET. The sea winds grow vicious. My bones ache, but I still train in the courtyard barefoot, under the lashing rain, letting the cold needles bite me into clarity.

He passes me sometimes. Our eyes meet, but there are no words.

I've come to crave that between us.

One night, it all changes.

I'm walking back from town, a bag of supplies slung over my shoulder, when I see a figure blocking the gate.

It's the uncle I stopped calling uncle years ago.

He's drunk. Smiling that smile I grew up dreading. The one that always came before the hurt.

"Look at you," he slurs. "All grown up. Think you can hide from me, little rat?"

I don't answer.

His hand reaches out, filthy, groping.

This time, I don't even think.

I break his jaw with the heel of my palm.

My kicks land harder than I ever thought possible. I hear his ribs break.

There is blood on my shoes. His breath stops before mine does.

I call the police on my phone. I give myself up.

The municipal jail is gray and stinking and rusty.

I sit on the wooden bench, my hands still stained red, my knuckles swollen. The guards don't ask questions.

The woman in a miniskirt across from me in the cell looks at me with a respectful nod and asks if she could braid my hair. I say yes.

I don't tell her my story, but she tells me I remind her of her daughter. The one who left her after losing a battle with dengue. We'd be about the same age now, she says. We even have the same texture hair.

I don't cry, but I let her.

I watch the woman doze off. I slide to the floor and lean against the sticky wall, hoping I could at least rest my burning eyes.

Even then all I think of is the dojo. The lashing rain. Him.

It's dawn when the cell door creaks open.

A young officer gestures for me to stand up and get out. The woman next to me is still fast asleep.

I rise to my feet. My whole body shakes.

I see him standing just outside.

He doesn't even look at me, but I know he's there for me.

The only solid and real thing in my life.

The local police chief is shaking his hand, refers to him as "Mr. Villarete."

We walk out of the station together, across the municipal

plaza where his multicab is parked. The sky is gray. The wind bites. The world looks damp and worn.

"Did you put towels by the eastern window?" I ask him suddenly.

He shakes his head. "I forgot."

I sigh. "It's okay. I'll mop it when I get home. I—"

"Cassandra." He never calls me by anything other than my real name. He inhales deeply before continuing. "Are you okay?"

I nod, facing him. My breath clouds between us. My voice cracks as I say, "Why did you come?"

He reaches up.

His hand is warm as it brushes my cheek tenderly, carefully.

"Because you fought back," he says.

That's when I kiss him.

Not out of want. Not at first.

Out of everything else. Pain. Loss. The ashes of stolen girlhood, reborn in his care.

But when he kisses me back, it's like a typhoon unravels inside me. It feels like my sorrow has teeth, and his lips are forgiveness.

We spend the night together, on his mats.

I finally call him by his name, "Anthony."

When I wake up the next morning, he is gone.

The dojo is still there, but it is hollow.

He left no note. No goodbye.

Just…absence.

And the mist of him.

# CHAPTER 4

## The Courtyard

Y EARS LATER, I STAND BAREFOOT IN MY COURTYARD. The gray walls still stand. I repainted them with my own hands.

Children run through the rain-soaked courtyard, laughter ringing off the stone. They swing sticks too big for their arms, shout like they're fighting dragons.

And I let them. Then I will teach them how to be still.

How to breathe. How to rise.

How to rise again after they fall.

I will teach them how to survive without apology.

On my desk, there's a photo. Black and white, grainy with time. It's the only one I have of him.

Eyes like mist. Face like stone. Hands as gentle as the breeze, as strong as the wind.

I trace his face every night. I talk to him often.

But I never saw him again.

But sometimes, when the mist rolls in thick and the ocean before me tastes like salt and promise, I feel him near.

And I smile.

I'll never be alone. I'll never be afraid anymore.

Because I carry him in my bones, in my breath.

In the way I move. In the way I teach.

Because the blood in my veins still remembers the Master that welcomed me home from the mist.

And his kiss that saved me.

# RAIN CHECK

# CHAPTER 1

## Strong Winds

I**T ALWAYS STARTS THE SAME.**

The storm barrels in sudden and merciless, rattling the glass windows of the stores of the old commercial building. The wind howls, a large gust sending my umbrella to the side, bent and useless against the raging downpour.

Rain slaps against my skin as I make my way to the corner convenience store. I try to wrestle my umbrella back into place, but I'm already soaked through, shivering as thunder cracks overhead.

I realize the umbrella is broken. I've taped it back together in a few places before, but now the plastic has snapped clean through. Sighing, I toss it into an overflowing garbage can. I tell myself to buy a stronger one next time, but it also means skipping meals for a few days.

By the time I push through the glass doors of the store, I look half-drowned.

And he's there. As always.

I know him as Danny.

I heard a little old lady call him by the name once, while she was buying Vicks and some lozenges.

He's maybe thirty-something, lean and tall, bronze skin glistening where his sleeves are rolled up. He has tousled dark hair he never bothers taming, and eyes so dark they sometimes flash gray in the store's light. Tattoos run along his arms, half hidden by his shirt, dangerous and beautiful all at once.

He looks up from behind the counter, and something in me tightens out of instinct.

My heart pounds, nipples straining under my wet blouse, my body betraying just how much I ache for his attention. I tell myself I only duck into this shop for shelter as I await the mercy of the rideshare or taxi service to take me home.

But the truth is, I always find my way here because of him.

He grabs a towel from under the counter and holds it out without a word. Swallowing hard, I reach for it a little too quickly. When my fingers brush his, heat sparks through me, sharper than the storm.

"Thanks," I manage, hoping he couldn't hear my voice shaking.

This is the fourth time he has done this in the past two months, since I started seeking shelter at his store whenever it rains after my night classes at the College of Law.

"No problem." In contrast to mine, his voice is steady and low-pitched. He slides a paper cup across the counter. "Coffee. On the house. With sugar, right?"

I nod and smile despite myself, wrapping both hands around the cup. The warmth seeps into my chilled fingers.

"You don't even know my name, and now you're giving me free coffee?"

"Then maybe you should tell me," he says, leaning just slightly closer.

"Alya," I answer, more breathless than I mean to be.

"Alya." His lips quirk as he repeats the word. "I'm Danny. Pay me back when the sun comes out. Rain check."

I always come to the store at night, but I don't argue.

"Rain check," I echo instead. "Fine."

The heat of the coffee spreads through me, but it's nothing compared to the heat pooling low in my belly from the way he's looking at me. His gaze doesn't wander crudely, but it lingers heavily.

I bring the coffee to my lips, because I need the excuse not to drown in his black-gray eyes. My eyes almost flutter close at how good it tastes.

"Guess I owe you a lot already," I say.

"You don't," he murmurs. "The storms have been brutal lately. A place like this is meant for shelter, anyway. Besides, everyone in the city knows where Montalban Mini Mart is. Easier for your ride to find you."

I meet his eyes. He's looking straight at me, not even blinking. I square my shoulders, trying in vain to push down the blush creeping up my neck. "Still. You didn't have to."

He grabs a black plastic packet from under the counter. He slides it toward me. When I touch it, I realize it's a pair of rubber slippers.

"You're going to wreck those shoes if you go home like that," he says softly.

This time, the blush sets my entire face on fire. "You don't have to do that."

"Only for regulars," he replies smoothly. "You've been in here enough times to qualify."

I bend my head down to hide my face, pretending to set my coffee and bag down on the counter. I slide my feet out of the soaked flats and ease them into the slippers.

"Feels like cheating," I say. "You're giving me too much."

When I look up, he hands me a small bottle of water, shrugging as he says, "Hydrate."

I stare at him, more surprised now than flustered. I want to ask him why he's doing all this. Why he notices my needs when no one else ever does.

Instead, I say, "You're…strangely prepared for rescuing half-drowned strangers."

He chuckles. "Not strangers anymore, Alya."

The sound almost undoes me, so I try to gather myself and do the only thing I could. The one thing he deserves.

I smile.

"No, Danny," I say. "Not strangers anymore."

He smiles right back, and my breath stops for a second.

"Good," he says. "Makes it easier when you show up again next time."

I incline my head, amused at his statement. "What makes you think I will?"

"Because the rain always comes back," he says simply. His gaze holds mine a beat too long. "And so do you."

I feel the flush in my face coming back full force. Just then, my phone pings, letting me know that the driver has reached the store.

I mutter *goodnight* and *thank you*, grabbing my bag, water bottle, and coffee as I go. I don't wait for him to answer.

Because he's right.

I'll be back. He knows it. I know too.

That's how it starts. Towels and coffee. Then he's added slippers and water.

His quiet care. My reckless need to be near him when the world around me is dark and drenched.

And now, the storm is raging louder inside me than outside.

# CHAPTER 2

*Storm Signal*

**J**UST LIKE ALWAYS, SHE APPEARS.

The moment the rain hits like a hammer against the glass, I know Alya will be at my door sooner than later.

She's gentle-looking and soft-spoken, but I can always see the steel flickering behind her eyes like lightning. She always looks put together even during the heaviest storms, dressed in bright-colored blouses and skirts.

Tonight, as she walks through the glass doors, her long dark hair hangs loose, dripping down her shoulders. Her light brown skin gleams wet under the fluorescent glow. Her umbrella hangs limp and loose from her right hand.

She shivers as she hobbles in, and I'm already reaching for the towel.

"Here," I say without preamble.

"Hi," she says as she takes it. "Me again. Thanks."

Her fingers brush mine, and it's enough to send a shudder straight through me, even though I'm comparatively warm and dry. I grab a paper cup and dispense the coffee from the machine the way she always takes it. As I wait for the cup to fill, I gesture toward the plastic stool I had set up by the counter.

"Sit. Dry off. You waiting for a ride?"

She nods, smiling faintly as she sets down her bag and umbrella on the floor, where I had also set up some hand-woven rugs to keep the surface dry and slippage-free.

"Yeah," she answers. "App says twenty to thirty minutes. I'll try not to flood your floor in the meantime. I like these mats you brought in, by the way. Very colorful."

I nod. "I got them from the market last Sunday. Scraps from tailoring shops, I believe. You seem to like colors, so I took a chance on the brightest-looking ones."

She blushes as she wraps the towel around her shoulders, then averts her eyes to take her coffee from the counter.

"Well, they're very pretty," she says. "I really like them."

"Glad you do," I answer.

She settles on the stool, still not looking at me.

Her voice is soft but curious when she finally speaks. "This store…it's been here a long time, hasn't it? Feels older than the others on this block. I remember it being around when I first came to the city."

"Yeah," I admit. "One of the oldest in town. My grandparents opened it, then my dad and mom took over eventually. It was supposed to go to my brother, Eddie. He… passed away a while back. So here I am."

Her expression shifts as she looks at me, sympathy threading through her features, but it isn't pity. "I'm sorry. That must have been hard."

I nod. "It was. Still is. But the store's all I've got of my family, so I keep it running. Some of the employees have been with us for decades too."

She tilts her head, studying me. "So you're on your own then."

"I am." The words sit heavy on my tongue. "You?"

She takes a deep breath, as if weighing whether or not to say it. "Me too." Her eyes drop to her hands clutching the cup. "My father…he died years ago."

I don't speak, just wait. She glances at me, then looks away, words spilling like the rain outside.

"We had a farm in the province. He borrowed money from a rich businessman so I could go to college. Put the land up as collateral. He didn't really understand the documents. The businessman who wanted the land…they made sure of that. Well, there were typhoons that pretty much took all our harvests and my father missed more than a few payments. That was that. When they took everything—he couldn't live with it."

Her voice breaks. "My mother found him in the fields. He shot himself through the mouth with his *paltik*."

The breath I let out is ragged. "Alya…"

She shakes her head quickly. "My mother…she lasted a few months. Then a stroke. But I think she was already gone by then." She gives a shaky, humorless laugh. "I was lucky I had an aunt here in the city. She worked at a private school, got me a job in Admin when I finished college. She died two years ago."

Silence stretches between us, broken only by the hum of the refrigerators and the rain battering the glass.

Finally, I ask quietly, "And now?"

"Now it's just me." She lifts her chin, her voice steadier now. "I work days at the school. Go to law classes at night. I go to the college two blocks away. That's why I always find my way here."

"Law school," I echo. "That's no small thing."

Her smile is small, but fierce. "Someday I want to help people like my father. People who don't know the words on those papers. Who sign their lives away because no one explained it to them." Her eyes glisten, but her voice is hard and determined. "I won't let that happen again."

She's so damn brave it hurts. She's so damn *everything* it hurts.

"You're stronger than anyone I know," I tell her honestly.

Her phone pings, cutting through the moment. She glances down, then forces a smile. "My ride's here."

She stands up and hands me her empty cup and the towel back with a grateful nod. After gathering her bag and umbrella, she looks straight at me, eyes still bright with unshed tears.

"You've brought me good luck, you know," she says quietly. "I feel safe in your store. Every time I'm in here, I always manage to get a ride."

I walk her out into the storm, using one of the store's large umbrellas that we keep in our utility closet. The car idles at the curb, headlights slicing through the rain.

Alya pauses, then turns toward me, so close I can feel her heat through the chill.

Her eyes search mine, and before I can speak, she rises on her toes and kisses me.

It's not soft.

It's hungry.

Her lips part against mine, demanding and promising at the same time. A groan rips out of me before I can stop it, my free hand finding her waist, pulling her against me, every inch of her wet body molding to mine.

The kiss is lightning and thunder and everything I've been holding back for weeks since I first laid eyes on her.

She pulls back, breathless, lips swollen. Her smile trembles, but it's real. "Goodnight, Danny. Thanks for everything."

And then she's gone, slipping into the car, leaving me standing in the downpour with my umbrella, pulse hammering, the taste of her still burning in my mouth.

As I watch her disappear into the rain-drenched night, I already know.

I won't survive another storm without her.

# CHAPTER 3

## *Secret Heat*

**I**T ISN'T RAINING TONIGHT.

The air is still heavy with the day's heat, the sky streaked with thin clouds and the faintest shimmer of stars. It feels weird, walking to Danny's store without a storm pushing me toward it.

My heart beats fast, not from thunder this time, but from nerves. It's payday. I wanted to say thank you. And maybe…I just wanted to see him.

The plastic bag swings in my hand, warm with the weight of fried chicken and mixed meat noodles. I had to wait longer than expected at the restaurant nearby, and panic flutters in me as I hurry down the block.

What if he's already closed up?

What if I miss him?

But the store's lights glow steady. And when I push through the door, he's there.

Like always.

His head lifts, eyes catching mine. That dark, storm-gray gaze pins me.

The first thing he says makes me laugh, breathless with relief.

"It's not raining." His voice rumbles low, a smile forming on his lips as he speaks. "Are you okay?"

I nod, lifting the bag. "I brought dinner. To say thank you."

His smile curves wider, and something inside me falls—falls hard. Right then, I know I'm gone for him. Entirely.

"Dinner, huh?" He chuckles, a sound I want to trap and keep forever. "Guess I should get plates."

He moves to the tiny back office and returns with two mismatched plates and a pair of forks. He takes two cans of iced tea from the fridge and sets them up on the counter, next to where I have laid out the platters of chicken and noodles.

We sit and eat side by side, sharing food and warmth. Outside, the street is silent and still in the late evening. For a moment, it all feels almost ordinary.

"So," I venture, twirling noodles around my fork. "What about before the store? Before you took it over. Did you ever want to do something else?"

His jaw works, but the rest of him stills. "That's a loaded question."

I lean in, heart pounding. "I want to know, Danny. All of it. Whatever you'll tell me."

He sets down his fork, leans back, and breathes out slowly.

His voice is low as he speaks. "I was in prison. Got out a few years ago."

My chest tightens. "Prison? Why?"

His gaze locks on mine, his face expressionless. "Because I killed people. Four of them. For Eddie."

The room lurches, but I force myself to stay still.

"Your brother?" My voice cracks.

"Yeah." His voice roughens, cracking like thin glass under heavy weight. "Eddie was the golden one. Kind, steady, responsible. Took care of me when I was raising hell. Racing bikes, picking fights, wasting time. I was a joke to most people back then. Maybe I still am."

He pauses, dragging a hand down his face. "He was only two years older, but he was always there to pull me back. Keep me going in the right direction. He was my best friend."

I don't say anything when he stops speaking. Somehow, I know he's not done.

"One night, he was walking home after inventory," Danny continues. "Four guys jumped him. Took his money, his phone, his watch. And they stabbed him. Left him bleeding in the street like he was nothing. Knowing Eddie, he would have just given them what they wanted. He would not have put up a fight…unlike me."

A lump forms in my throat, hot and painful. "Oh, God…"

He goes on, his face unchanging. But his voice drops to something that sounds almost fragile.

"My parents were never the same after that. My dad even considered closing this store once, but his friends talked him out of it. And me?" His jaw flexes at the word. "I found them, Alya. Every last one of them. I killed them. One by one. Until there was no one left."

His eyes blaze with a pain that won't burn out, and I watch him, entranced.

"The police caught me after the fourth. I didn't fight it. My lawyer, one of Eddie's closest friends, got me a reduced sentence. I did my years. Got out on parole for good behavior."

He rolls up his sleeve, revealing the ink curling along his arm. "These? From my block. The guards called it Revenge Block. We're the guys who finished the jobs that other people couldn't. Not even our brave boys in blue."

"I was the *mayor* of the provincial jail for a while. It means I survived. You could say I even…thrived."

He looks at me closely, unblinking. "That's why I have the deepest respect for lawyers. If not for one, I could have just rotted away in prison. Because of Attorney Fabregas, I made it back out. Alone, but free for the most part."

I stare, unable to stop the flood of tears. My chest feels split wide open, raw and aching deeply.

"And your parents?" I manage to choke out.

He shakes his head slowly. "Gone before I got out. I came home to nothing but this store." His breath is ragged. "It's all I have left of my family. So I keep it alive. For Eddie. For my parents."

Danny reaches out, his fingers brushing my cheek with a tender hand. "And now…you're here with me." A wistful smile plays at the corners of his lips, the light slowly coming back into his eyes.

The fork slides from my hand, clattering against porcelain. I push back my chair and cross the small space to him. My arms go around his shoulders, holding him tight. He stiffens at first, then exhales.

"I guess you can say I'm lucky, too," he says softly. "Right?"

His arms wrap me up, crushing me against him. His face presses into my neck, hot breath shuddering against my skin.

He smells like soap, rain, and something darker and more dangerous. It only makes me hold him tighter. His heart hammers against mine, and I feel every ounce of his own storm breaking open.

"You're not alone," I say, voice thick with tears. "I'm here."

His grip tightens like he'll never let me go. And then, slowly, he pulls back, just enough to look at me. His eyes burn right into mine, silvery and glittering. My breath catches at the sight.

Before I can speak, his mouth is on mine.

It's rough and desperate, his lips devouring me like he's been starving for years. A cry escapes me, muffled against his mouth as his hands slide lower, gripping my hips, dragging me onto his lap.

I straddle him without thought, the stool creaking under us as his hands cup my butt, squeezing hard enough to make me gasp. Heat sears through me, pooling low and hot in my stomach, my nipples hardening under my blouse as he presses me closer to him.

"Danny," I whisper against his lips, shuddering as his tongue sweeps into my mouth.

He groans raggedly, and grinds me down against the hard length straining through his jeans.

"You drive me crazy," he rasps. "Every damn time."

I clutch his shoulders, dizzy with need, and kiss him back like I'll never get another chance. Tears and hunger blur together, heartbreak turning into fire, into something I can't fight anymore.

I don't ever want to.

He groans low in his chest, and suddenly his hands are on my waist. He lifts and sets me down on the counter with a roughness that makes me squeal in surprise. The plates rattle, one tips over and clatters to the floor, but neither of us cares.

He reaches beneath my blouse, palms tracing their way over the bare skin of my stomach until his hands cup my breasts under my bra, his thumbs rubbing the nipples in slow circles, making me writhe against him.

"Alya." My name leaves him hoarsely. "Tell me to stop. Tell me and I'll stop."

My hands cup his face, trembling but certain. "Don't stop."

"*Fuck*," he says raggedly. "I'm starving. I'm starving for you."

His hands go lower, down my waist, then moves along my thighs, pushing them open. Then his mouth is on mine again, his hands dragging my skirt higher, higher, until I'm trembling with the exposure, the danger, the need. He kisses down my jaw, my throat, the frantic rise of my chest. Each brush of his lips breaks me open, until I'm shaking, until I can't think.

"Danny," I whisper as he slides off my panties.

"It's okay," he answers. "I've got you. I've always got you."

Then his hand takes over. He caresses and rubs, fingers stroking and moving in and out of me, gently at first, then with more urgency. Under his touch, I feel my body come alive, warm and wet and wanting.

When his head lowers further, his eyes meet mine, dark and burning, asking without words. My answer is in the way I arch toward him, in the way my fingers tangle in his hair.

And then his mouth claims me.

The shock of it rips a cry from my throat, sharp and unrestrained, echoing throughout the store. My body jolts, my knees clamping instinctively around his shoulders, but his grip is firm, holding me wide for him. The first stroke of his tongue is scorching, every nerve in me coming alive.

"Danny—" My voice breaks, begging for more as I lift my hips toward the release that his tongue and lips are promising.

He moans against me, the sound vibrating through every inch of my body, and it undoes me. I tip my head back, clutching fistfuls of his hair, legs jerking helplessly as he devours me. Heat floods in my belly, building fast, too fast, until I'm whimpering his name.

"You taste like heaven," he rasps against me. "You were made for me, Alya. My own heaven."

And then I'm gone, breaking against his mouth, sobbing and gasping for air, every ounce of me ripping into pieces under him. He holds me through it, his hands strong on my thighs, his lips and tongue relentless as he finishes me off, until I collapse back on the counter.

When he finally lifts his head, his lips are slick, his eyes blazing and tender all at once. He kisses my inner thigh, then my knee, then he finally rises.

I'm still shaking when his chin lands above my head, his lips brushing against my hair. His arms cage me on the counter, his breath hot against my cheek, his chest rising and falling.

He's breathing as hard as I am, voice raw when he mutters, "I've been starving, Alya. And I'll never get enough of you."

And I know I'm lost.

I know I am completely, irrevocably his.

That's when it hits me.

He hasn't had anything. He gave me everything, and he's still burning.

His hunger presses against me where our bodies touch.

Now I want to feed him, to take care of him, the same way he just took care of me.

Before I lose my nerve, I slide down from the counter, using his shoulders to pull myself down. My knees sink into the rugs on the floor.

He freezes above me, his eyes going wide. "Alya, you don't have to—"

"I want to," I cut him off, my voice shaky but certain. My hands rest on his thighs, feeling the heat of him through denim. My heart pounds so hard I can barely breathe. "I've never…done this before. But I want to. For you."

He groans, rubbing his hands over his face like he's fighting himself. "Christ. You're gonna kill me."

I swallow hard, fingers fumbling as I push him toward the counter. I feel clumsy and terrified, but determined. His hands hover near my face, as if he's afraid to touch me and afraid to let me go at the same time. When I unzip him and pull down his jeans and briefs, he shudders like the world just cracked open.

Then I see the length of him, rock-hard and red and starving for me. My hands close around him, then I take him into my mouth.

His head tips back, a broken sound ripping from his chest. "Oh, God, Alya…"

Every reaction of his—every gasp, every ragged moan, every jerk of his hips—ignites me. I've never felt power like this, never felt someone come undone because of me. He digs his hands in the counter behind him, muscles locked, body shaking.

I keep going, using my hands, my tongue, my lips, finding a rhythm, my nervousness fading under the rawness of his need. The way he curses under his breath, the way my name falls from his lips—it all makes me braver.

"You have no idea," he gasps out, his hands moving to my hair and his hips starting to thrust in time with my mouth, "what you're doing to me."

The sound of his voice, thick with devastation and desire, makes me feel light-headed. My hands clutch tighter, my whole body humming with heat as I give him everything I can.

And when he finally breaks, when his control shatters and he groans my name like it's the only word he knows, I feel it through every inch of me.

His release is raw, almost violent, but his hands cup my face after, tender and trembling, pulling me up into his arms.

He kisses me almost reverently. "You…you're everything. I don't deserve you, but God help me, I'll never let you go."

I'm breathless and shaking, lips swollen and heart burning, and all I can think is…

I don't want him to.

# CHAPTER 4

## *Sky Falling*

THE STORM HASN'T STOPPED SINCE SUNDOWN.
Rain pours relentlessly over the city, rivers crawling down the street, floodwater creeping past the gutters. I ask Willie, the young stockboy who had taken over from his father, to drop off the old cashier, Carmen, and go on straight home. I tell them we might not even open the store in the morning.

They fuss about me staying and tell me to go home, too, but I wave them off. This isn't the first time I've ridden out a storm alone.

But tonight isn't like every other night.

It's past seven. My eyes keep flicking to the clock, then the door. Alya's classes don't finish until nine, but already my chest is tight, almost restless.

Two nights ago, she brought me dinner and nearly broke me open on the counter with her warmth, her kiss, her touch.

With all of her.

The way she held me after, as if I was worth saving.

I didn't ask for more. I just made sure she got into a car

safely before I locked up. But the taste and the feel of her has been burning in me since.

I wait. I pace. The minutes crawl, and the storm only grows worse.

By fifteen past nine, my hands dig into the counter, the same place where I had lifted and stripped and tasted her only nights ago.

But still no Alya.

By half past nine, my pulse is thundering louder than the rain. Rage and fear coil together until I can't sit still another second.

Then the power flickers—and dies.

The store sinks into blackness, thunder splitting the sky. "Fuck this."

I grab my phone, its glow cutting a pale circle in the dark. I don't hesitate anymore. I lock up fast, splash into the street, the water cold and rising around my boots.

The city is empty. Shuttered shops, no cars, no people. Just storm and silence. I run hard, water slapping up to my calves, until I reach the alley down the block. The garage door groans as I haul it open. My bike waits in the shadows, untouched for months.

"C'mon, baby," I mutter, swinging my leg over. The engine coughs, then roars, vibrating through me. I gun the throttle, spray kicking up as I swerve into the drowned city.

The streets are blacked out, water up to the hubs, but the machine growls steady beneath me.

I ride toward the college, headlights slicing through thick sheets of rain. Every block feels endless. My chest aches with the thought of her out there alone, soaked and cold. By the time I see the faint silhouette of the waiting shed in front of the campus, my heart nearly rips through my ribs.

There she is.

Alya is huddled under the crooked roof, rain tearing at her broken umbrella, water rushing ankle-deep around her. Her hair is plastered to her face, her bag clutched to her chest, but she's still standing.

Still fighting.

The second she sees me, her lips curve in the smallest, fiercest smile.

"I'm glad you came." Her voice is shaky but strong. "The water was too deep to get through to your shop. And no drivers would take me. Said the flood was too high."

I kill the engine, splashing to a stop, water soaking through my clothes.

"It's okay," I rasp, swinging off the bike. "This motorcycle's tough. It can take a little water."

But I don't give her the chance to say more. I reach her, grab her, drag her against me with a force that's half desperation, half relief. My arms wrap her up tightly.

She gasps against my chest. "Danny, I—"

I cut her off with my mouth. The kiss is wild, rain-slick, teeth and tongue and heat. She tastes like storm and survival, and I drink her down. Her hands clutch at my shirt, holding me just as hard, answering every ounce of my hunger with her own.

When I manage to tear myself away to speak, I don't let her go.

"You're not alone anymore. You hear me? You've got me. Always."

Her eyes shine in the pale light, wet from more than

the rain. She nods once, trembling, and pulls me down into another kiss.

This time, it feels like a promise in the middle of the drowned streets.

And I promise myself I'll burn the whole world before I let her stand alone again.

"Don't leave me alone," Alya whispers against my lips, her breath trembling. "Please, Danny. Don't ever leave me alone."

My hands cup her face, thumbs brushing away the rain streaming down her cheeks.

"I won't," I say. "I promise I won't."

"Maybe…this is where I belong," she says, eyes wide as she looks at me. "With you. That's why I keep coming back to the store whenever there's a storm. Because you're the only person I've ever met who makes me feel like I could never be hurt, even when the world is angry."

The confession cracks something inside me. She's shaking, but she keeps talking, almost like a lost girl finding her way home in the dark.

"The first time I saw you," she says, "you got me the coffee I wanted. And you refused my payment. You said 'Rain check, miss.'" Her lip trembles. "You always said it to me, but to me it meant…" Her voice trails off, then she takes a deep breath and continues. "It meant you would always welcome me back, even at my worst. That's why I just kept coming back to you, Danny. I didn't know where else to go."

I pull her against me, arms locking around her small, soaked frame, pressing her head to my chest. My throat is tight, my own eyes stinging. "Alya…"

She buries her face against me, words muffled. "You're the only place I've ever felt safe."

I lower my mouth to her ear. "Then let me take you home. Let me love you the way I've always wanted to."

She jerks back. "What?"

"I love you." My voice is hoarse but steady. "I've loved you from the first storm you walked into."

Her head shakes wildly, rain flying. "How can you say that? I'm nobody. I can't even afford an umbrella half the time. I don't have anything to give you, Danny."

I catch her chin, make her look at me. "No, Alya. I love you because *you* are everything. You're brave, strong, relentless. You walk through storms and still show up. You survived everything, and you're still here." My thumb strokes her cheek, then I trace its path with my lips. "And you're the most amazing and beautiful woman I've ever laid eyes on. You're my everything, even if you think otherwise. I guess I'll just spend the rest of my life trying to convince you."

Something in her breaks open at my words. She lets out a sob, then leaps up, wrapping her arms around my neck, clinging to me like she'll drown if she lets go. I hold her tight, burying my face in her wet hair.

"Take me home," she chokes out. "Get me out of here."

I scoop her up against me, her legs locking around my waist, and carry her to the bike. The engine roars back to life under us, headlights slicing through the flood as we surge into the rising water together.

For the first time in years, I don't feel alone.

# CHAPTER 5

*Shadow Story*

THE RAIN LASHES AGAINST MY FACE AS DANNY DRIVES us through the flooded streets, the motorcycle cutting through dark water.

My arms are wrapped tight around his waist, cheek pressed to his back. Every muscle in him hums with focus, but I can feel the way he eases closer whenever we hit a deeper patch. His body feels like a shield against the storm.

We reach the store's block, an older part of the city where buildings rise narrow and tall. He doesn't stop at the corner but keeps going instead, driving into a wide alley lined with steel gates, their courtyards inside half-drowned. He pulls into one, the engine rumbling low before he cuts it off. My ears ring with silence, except for the endless rain.

"This way," he says.

His hand finds mine and he leads me off the bike, through the arch of the courtyard, toward a worn staircase that creaks under our steps. The power's still out, the building sunk in darkness, but Danny lifts his phone, the small torch casting a pale halo over his face.

Shadows carve along his cheekbones, catching in the wet strands of his hair, and he looks younger somehow. Almost shy.

"This is the way things used to be done here," he says softly, his voice carrying in the stillness. "People lived above or beside their shops. My parents did."

The admission makes my heart tighten. He's always so solid, so strong and infallible, but right now, in the flickering light, I see the boy he once was, still living with ghosts.

The lock of the heavy wooden door clicks open, and he ushers me inside. The apartment smells faintly of wood and rain.

Danny sets his phone on a table and switches on two emergency lamps. The glow from them is warm enough, pushing back the dark.

The apartment is simple and clean, but old. Around me are cabinets with chipped handles, sofas with threadbare arms, and low tables with scratches. The floor is covered with patterned linoleum.

On the wall, framed photographs hang in careful lines. A couple, most likely his parents, smiling, their arms around each other. A boy who looks similar to Danny but with neater hair and calmer eyes, holding a trophy, his grin easy and kind.

Danny's voice is low as he follows my gaze. "That's Eddie. He always kept this place alive, even when I was being a pain in everyone's ass. My parents…they left it just the way it was. Can't imagine what it must have been like for them. Eddie gone. Then I was put away." He swallows, then looks back at me. "When I got out, I came back here. It still felt like home, even if they weren't around anymore."

He picks up one of the portable lamps, gesturing down

the narrow hall with his free hand. "The other rooms are empty. No one's lived in them since. Just me."

I follow him as he leads the way. He stops at a doorway at the end of the corridor.

"This is mine." He runs a hand through his wet hair and tries for a smile as he turns the knob and pushes the door open. "You can stay here as long as you want. No strings attached. Just…home."

The word echoes in me, deeper than I expect.

*Home.*

Light spills on a small space, with wooden floors and a surprisingly neat bed with white sheets. The walls are bare, lined on one side with worn cabinets. A few books are piled next to a small lamp on the nightstand.

It isn't grand, but it feels safe.

It feels real.

Danny clears his throat, almost awkward now, as he hands over the emergency lamp. Our fingers brush lightly, but he pulls back.

"I'll try to find something to eat. Might be cold, but it's better than nothing. I've got some clothes in the cabinet if you want to change."

He hesitates at the door, his hand on the frame. In the lamplight, his eyes are softer than I've ever seen them, uncertain. He looks like he's standing at the edge of something he never thought he'd share.

"Get comfortable," he says quietly. "I'll be right outside."

The door shuts behind him, leaving me in the dim glow, my heart pounding.

Then it hits me with the force of the storm outside.

This man, this room, this night…it's all a revelation.

For the first time in years, I feel like I might finally belong somewhere.

$\backsim$

The light never comes back on.

The storm presses against the windows, heavy and loud, the rain a constant roar. I move carefully by the glow of the emergency lamp Danny left me.

I peel off my wet clothes, shivering as I pour water from the bathroom bucket over myself. It's cold, but it clears the storm from my skin. I wash off the taste of fear, the weight of the street.

I towel off, then rummage through his cabinet until I find a pair of old shorts and a plain shirt that hang loose on me but still smell faintly of him.

When I open the door, the hall is aglow with lamplight. Not the chargeable battery lamps from earlier, but real kerosene lamps, their flames flickering gold.

Danny glances up from the table. He's changed, too, into a fresh white shirt and loose dark shorts. His hair is damp, curling at the ends.

"These used to belong to my grandparents," he says, almost shyly, tilting his head toward the lamps on the table. "Everyone had something like this in the old days, I guess."

On the six-seat dining table between us, there are bottles of water and two steaming cups of noodles.

He nods toward a chair. "Not much of a feast, but it's hot. I've got some more boiled water if you want to have coffee later."

We eat in silence at first, rain filling the spaces between

our words. Then small talk slips in. We talk about harmless things. The taste of the broth. The memory of storms past and how the building and the store survived then.

He doesn't touch me. Not once.

It surprises me. After everything, after what happened on the counter, I thought…

But maybe he's holding back. Maybe he doesn't want to break whatever this fragile, impossible thing between us is.

When we finish, he gathers the cups and bottles, moving to clean up.

I watch him in the lamplight. Broad shoulders, wet hair, careful hands, the quiet patience in him…and I can't take it anymore.

I cross the room and press myself against his back, my arms sliding around his waist. He freezes, then slowly turns, setting the dishes aside.

He bends to kiss my forehead, his lips lingering there. "You should rest," he murmurs. "Do you need paracetamol? You've been through a lot tonight."

I shake my head. "No."

He exhales, half a laugh, half in what seems to be disbelief. "I still can't believe you're here. That you're with me and…" His voice falters.

I nod, cutting him off. "Put it away, Danny. All of it. The worry. The doubt. Because yes. I'm here. We're both here. We're home. And I belong with you."

And I see it in his eyes.

The control he's been gripping slips loose. His hands are suddenly on my face, his mouth crashing to mine with a hunger that steals my breath.

The kiss is wild and desperate. I gasp as his hands slide

down, gripping my hips, my ass, hauling me up against him. His body is hard and unyielding, his groan tearing through the quiet.

We stumble, then fall together onto the floor, the linoleum cold under my back, his weight pressing me down. His hands are everywhere—palming, clutching, greedy— as he tears my borrowed shirt up over my head and drags my shorts down my legs, stripping me bare in the flickering lamplight.

I arch, helpless beneath him, naked and trembling. His mouth breaks from mine only to trail down my throat, my chest, lower still, until his breath sears hot against the most fragile part of me.

"Danny…" My voice is a soft, pleading cry.

His eyes lift, molten gray in the golden glow.

"Mine," he growls. "You're mine, Alya."

Then he bends and devours me, and the storm outside has nothing on the storm that breaks inside me.

Danny's mouth pulls me apart until I'm shaking, until every breath is a whimper. My body still hums when I reach for him, tugging at his shirt.

"Let me," I whisper, hands clumsy, but more determined than ever.

His eyes darken, breath catching as I peel his shirt away. My palms skim his chest, his skin hot and alive under my fingertips, muscles rippling like coiled ropes of strength. He's beautiful, ink curling down his arms and around his torso, scars etched faintly across his skin.

He's breathtakingly real, a man made of storms and survival.

I touch lower and lower, tentatively, and he groans,

catching my wrist but not pushing me away. His restraint shakes through him, but he lets me explore, lets me learn the shape of him with my hands.

"Alya," he rasps. "You don't—"

"Let me," I cut him off. "I want this."

My voice almost falters, but the truth in it steadies me as I pull down his shorts and briefs.

His control breaks. He leans down, kissing me hard, then softer, trailing over my cheek, my throat, my collarbone, his hands cupping my breasts, thumbs brushing over my hard nipples until I arch helplessly beneath him. His mouth follows, hot and hungry, worshipping me in ways that leave me gasping.

He lingers between my thighs, caressing and teasing and licking, until I'm undone again, pleading for him without words.

Then he stills.

Rain hammers the roof, thunder rolls, but his whisper cuts through everything.

"I love you, Alya."

My breath catches. "Danny, I—"

"I love you," he says again, fiercer this time. To my ears, it sounds like the only truth he's ever known. "From the first time I saw you walk into my store and my life. From the first rain check. Always."

Tears sting my eyes, mingling with sweat. I wrap my legs around him, pulling him closer, needing him. Needing this.

"Then take me," I breathe. "Because I love you too."

His mouth claims mine as he gently lowers himself over me. His hands cradle my face and stroke my hair as he slowly enters me. He lets me adjust, waiting patiently with kisses and soft, soothing whispers.

I clutch him tight as I feel him inside me, my body molding to his, then I begin to move. My hips meet his and he groans and curses, then he matches my rhythm with thrusts that become harder, faster, and more desperate.

The world narrows to the heat of his skin, the press of his chest, the worship in his eyes, the pleasure that sears throughout my body as he pounds into me.

His mouth finds my breasts, his name falls from my lips, and I give myself to him completely, wrapped around him as the night swallows us whole.

And in the darkness, in his arms, I finally understand what it means to be home.

# CHAPTER 6

## Stolen Kiss

THE STORM OUTSIDE DOESN'T LET UP, BUT INSIDE, I can't get enough of her.

Alya is under me, around me, trembling and fierce, and every time she gasps my name it's like a match striking inside my chest. I'm starving, and I know it shows in the way I kiss her, the way I can't stop touching her, the way I keep pulling her back when she tries to breathe.

We burn through the night, moving like the storm wind itself is chasing us. The linoleum floor becomes too small, so I lift her and set her on the table where we ate not an hour ago. The bowls and bottles scatter to the floor, and she laughs breathlessly before I swallow the sound with my mouth.

Her laughter, her tears, her cries—I take them all, because they're mine now, every one.

When the table groans, I carry her again, settling her on the sofa, sinking into the worn cushions with her spread across me, my hands holding her by the ankles as I take her more slowly, more deeply.

And when we're done that way, I ask her to get on top of me.

The flickering lamplight paints her skin gold, and I can't stop staring at her. Alya's hair is loose and wild around her, her eyes still heavy with need, her lips swollen, but she rides me like a goddess as I squeeze her breasts, surprisingly full for someone as petite as her. She leans down to kiss me, and I think I could die like this, drowning in her.

But even the sofa can't contain us. I press her gently against the wall, her body arching into mine, her nails digging into my back, and I whisper against her ear, "You're everything. Do you know that? You're everything."

She whispers it back, and the sound tears me apart. I pound into her harder, mouth lowering to take her nipple, and she cries out, rubbing up and down, taking every inch of pleasure I am giving her.

By the time I carry her into my room, we're both shaking, but I still want more. I set her down on my bed—the bed I've slept in alone for years, the bed my parents kept waiting for me while I was locked away—and tonight, it finally feels alive.

She looks at me, wide-eyed, uncertain but brave, as I bend her on all fours at the edge.

I know I have to show her. Not just what it means to be touched, but what it means to be loved completely.

Then I take her from behind, my hands going around to cup her breasts, my lips and teeth nipping at the back of her neck.

I guide her, teach her how to move with me, how to let go of the fear, how to give in to the hunger that's been between us since the first storm.

Every time she hesitates, I hold her. Every time she

falters, I kiss her. And when she grows bolder, when she learns the rhythm of us, I almost lose myself in the wonder of it.

We make love and fall together through the night, over and over, until the storm outside fades into the gray hush of dawn, until she collapses on top of me, her body tangled with mine, hair damp against my chest, breath warm on my skin. I stroke her back, slowly and lightly, as the sun begins to rise behind the curtains.

For the first time in years, I don't feel restless. I don't feel haunted. I feel…whole. Because Alya is in my arms, and she's never leaving.

I kiss the crown of her head, whispering into her hair as sleep finally drags me under.

"I love you. Always."

And she stirs against me, murmuring her answer, "I love you too."

༄

The first thing I notice is the quiet.

No pounding rain, no cracking thunder, no rushing water. Just the soft hum of a city wrung out by a storm.

Then I see her next to me.

Alya's curled into me, hair spread like ink across the pillow, her cheek pressed against my chest.

My arm is numb beneath her but I don't dare move. Not yet. I just watch. The rise and fall of her breath. The way she clutches the blanket like she's afraid it will slip away.

I've always woken up alone. In prison. In this apartment.

In silence. But now…now there's someone beside me. Someone warm. Someone real.

Someone I love.

Her lashes flutter, and then her eyes blink open, soft and sleepy, finding mine. For a second, we just stare at each shyly, like two kids caught doing something forbidden.

Then she gives me the smallest smile, and I'm done for.

"Good morning," she whispers.

"Good morning," I manage, my voice rough.

A sharp ping breaks the spell. She leans across me to grab her phone from the nightstand, the blanket slipping, her bare breast brushing my shoulder. I bite back a groan. She scans the screen, then laughs softly.

"School's closed. Flood's too bad in the city to go anywhere." She sets the phone down, looking back at me, eyes gleaming.

I raise a brow, smirking. "Well. Looks like you're stuck with me."

She giggles, light and unguarded. And before I can blink, she swings a leg over, straddling me. My breath leaves me in a rush.

"Alya…"

Her lips brush mine teasingly, then her tongue flicks out to trace my lower lip. "Rain check?"

Heat slams through me, shattering any control I thought I still had. I grip her hips, my head falling back against the pillow with a helpless laugh. "Hell, no."

She shifts her weight just enough to make me groan, her hair falling like a curtain around us. The blanket slides off her body, and her skin feels like warm silk against mine. My body responds before I can think, hard and aching beneath her.

Her smile tilts wickedly. She rocks once, very slowly, and I choke out a sound I haven't made in forever.

"You're a greedy goddess," I rasp, clutching her thighs, staring up at her like she's a vision I don't deserve.

Her eyes glimmer with mischief and fire. "Why else do you think I keep coming to you? Every single time?" She grinds again, teasing and tormenting. "I know what I want."

A curse breaks from my throat. My hands grip her harder, sliding up her waist, her back, her breasts, desperate not to lose my mind.

"You're killing me," I groan.

"No," she whispers as she leans down, her mouth ghosting over mine. "I'm keeping you alive."

And she's right. Every move from her body, every taunt in her voice, every kiss she steals…it's life itself.

A life we might just live in love, through whatever storms may come.

I surge up, sealing my mouth to hers, tasting her laugh, her moan—all of her. The blanket tangles, the room spins, and I know I'll never get enough.

I'm hers. Always.

No rain checks.

Not ever.

# SUNSETS IN SEPTEMBER

# CHAPTER 1

## *Another Year*

E VERY SEPTEMBER, I RETURN.

The pier is the same as it was the day he first brought me here.

The wooden planks are still weathered by salt, while sea spray still mists the air. I can still hear fishermen's laughter echoing down the rails.

My fiancé used to say this place feels like forever.

But forever never came.

He died in a highway accident three years ago.

But I still come on his birthday and stay for a few days. Every day I'm here, I sit at the edge of the pier with a paper cup of coffee, watch the sun burn the sea gold, and pretend he's beside me.

Only this year, I'm not alone.

There's a man standing at the rail, hands in his pockets, shoulders broad under a navy button-down. His presence is quiet but steady. He glances at me once—dark eyes, sharp looking but tired—and nods.

I nod back.

That's all. But it's enough to unsettle the rhythm of my ritual.

ↄ

The next evening, he's there again.

"Hi," he says, voice deep and even.

"Hi."

We stand side by side, not quite close but not far. He smells faintly of something cool and smoky.

On the third evening, he says, "You come here often?"

"Every September," I admit. "This is my third."

His lips twitch, like he understands more than I said. "My first time this year."

There's silence. The sea roars before us. I want to ask him why, but something in his face, one deeply etched with lines of time and loss, stops me.

We don't trade stories.

Just quiet nods, shared sunsets, and the small comfort of knowing someone else carries ghosts too.

# CHAPTER 2

## Another Ending

O N MY LAST NIGHT, THE PIER IS BUSIER THAN USUAL. The planks are packed with vendors selling grilled corn, peanuts, and balloons. Couples and families walk around leisurely, admiring the view at high tide, while kids run about barefoot. The promise of rain hangs heavy in the air.

I linger longer than usual, waiting for the sky to turn the color he loved, blazing orange fading into deep purple. It's like saying goodbye, in a way.

Another end to another year.

When I finally turn toward the narrow road leading back to town where my pension house is, I don't notice the man shadowing me until his hand snatches at my bag.

I stumble, shouting, clutching the strap as panic explodes in my chest.

Then suddenly, he's there.

The man from the pier.

Moving faster than I can blink, he twists the snatcher's

wrist, wrenches my bag free, and sends the thief stumbling into the sand. The snatcher curses and bolts into the dark.

I'm left gasping, clutching my bag, staring at him.

"Are you okay?" he asks, voice firm and steady.

"I…yes," I breathe out. "Yes. I think so."

He exhales, the coiled tension seemingly leaving his body. He pulls a badge from his back pocket and flashes it briefly. "I'm a cop. Senior Inspector Brian Medina."

It all clicks into place—the way he carries himself, the way he moved so quickly and effortlessly.

"I'm…Meera. Attorney Meera Fabregas."

He extends a hand, a little formally. "It's nice to meet you."

I take it, my palm disappearing underneath his. His grip is firm, but somehow gentle. "Nice to meet you too. Thanks for your help."

He shakes his head. "I'm sorry I wasn't able to reach him earlier. I could have caught him before he did that to you."

I stare at him. "Have you been…watching me?"

His jaw flexes. He hesitates for a moment before he answers.

"Yes. I wanted to make sure you were safe. From the first day."

 ᗡᴑ 

He offers to walk me to the pension house. We make our way together back toward town, taking the boardwalk route that skirts the beach.

My knees are still weak from the encounter, but his presence steadies me.

"Why September?" I ask finally, voice trembling.

His silence is long. Then, he says softly, "It's my wife's birthday yesterday. She passed away almost two years ago. Cancer." His tone is matter-of-fact, but his eyes are raw. "I came here because this place was her favorite view. We had our honeymoon in a resort nearby. She used to say sunsets made her believe in happy endings. Riding off into the sunset, all that. She owned a flower shop."

I swallow hard. "My fiancé loved sunsets too. He…he died in a crash. I work in the city, but I come back for his birthday. This is his hometown. And the pier was where he proposed to me."

We stop walking. For the first time, we truly face each other. Two people bound by grief, standing in the golden afterglow of a sun that refuses to linger.

"I'm sorry for your loss," he says.

"I'm sorry for your loss, too," I echo quietly. "Your wife sounds like a wonderful lady."

He gives me a small, sad smile. "You could say she was a romantic."

I smile. "She's right. We didn't get our happy endings, but sunsets do make you believe in them. They're always something to look forward to, in spite of everything."

He nods. "They're like second chances, I guess."

I look at the darkening horizon, then at him, tilting my head. "You can say that. I believe in second chances. Maybe that's why I became a lawyer."

Neither of us say anything for several long moments, then I take a deep breath and continue. A part of me wants him to know. To understand.

"Years ago, a very good friend of mine was killed in a

robbery. His brother found the men who did it and finished them all off. I knew he did what he did out of love, so I did everything I could to make sure he got out of prison early. He and his wife have a son now. She's going to take the Bar exams next year. Hopefully she'll become a lawyer too."

Brian leans over and takes my chin in his hand. "I have never heard of anything more romantic than that, coming from a lawyer."

I laugh, blushing at this new, strange kind of connection. "Look at us. Old romantics."

I find myself caught by the way his eyes soften when they rest on me as he moves closer.

It's not pity, but recognition. A mirror of everything I've carried alone.

I don't know who moved first, but when his lips touch mine, it isn't fire at first.

It's a spark, cautious and waiting.

He's giving me time to pull away. To say no.

But I kiss him back. Harder.

And that's when the spark catches.

He groans low in his throat, one hand rising to cradle my cheek, the other moving around my waist to pull me closer. His thumb brushes my skin gently, even as his mouth moves with growing urgency against mine.

I clutch his shirt tightly, panting, and ask, "Do you want to come with me? For coffee?"

Just as breathlessly, he answers, "Yes."

# CHAPTER 3

## Another Beginning

MY LEGS DON'T STOP SHAKING, EVEN WHEN WE REACH my room at the pension house.

My fingers fumble the keys, but his hand covers mine, steady and firm, guiding the door open. He reaches up to flip on the light, a soft golden glow settling over the tiny space.

Inside, it feels too quiet. Too small. My pulse won't slow.

I set my bag down on the table, my breath still ragged.

I turn and look at him standing at the threshold—the buttons at his collar undone, the storm still raging in his eyes—and I realize exactly what I feel.

It's something I haven't felt in years. Something I never gave myself the permission to feel again.

It's want. It's need.

And it's the last thing from coffee.

Because it's him.

The door clicks shut behind him, and suddenly it's just us and the sound of the sea, muffled through the open window.

The words escape before I can stop them.

"I don't want to be alone tonight, Brian."

His silence is heavy, eyes locking onto mine. Then he steps closer, close enough that I feel his heat.

"Neither do I."

The kiss is molten, a clash of everything unsaid, a dam of the years breaking wide open.

His mouth claims mine with burning heat, his hands anchoring my waist. I gasp against him, and he deepens it, tongue sliding past my lips, tasting me.

I clutch at his shirt, feeling the solid muscle beneath, the tension coiled and breaking free. He lifts me easily, settling me on the edge of the bed without breaking the kiss.

"Meera," he murmurs against my throat. His hand slides down my arm, to my waist, pausing as if to ask permission. "Tell me if you want this. If not, I'll leave."

"Yes," I answer, arching into his touch. "I want this. I want you."

I shiver as he starts to bare my body, not just the skin but the parts of myself I've hidden for years. He pauses, eyes dark as he takes in the sight of my breasts, still partially covered by my lace bra.

"You're beautiful, Meera," he says, as if it's the simplest truth.

My throat tightens. I don't remember the last time anyone looked at me this way.

He undresses me slowly, kissing each new stretch of skin. When his palm cups my bare breasts then moves to the heat between my legs, and when his mouth follows, I gasp out his name again and again, clutching his shoulders.

He doesn't stop there. His lips trail fire on my skin, then he slides lower, pushing my legs apart.

"You're so beautiful," he says again, voice gravelly with desire. "I want to taste all of you."

"Brian…" My eyes widen, and I almost scream when his mouth finds me.

But he is as steady as the tide.

His tongue and lips move relentlessly over that achingly wet part of me, flicking and swirling in maddening rhythm. His fingers follow, and I come undone, legs shooting into the air as he licks me clean, even as I shake and whimper under his touch.

His clothes come off then, one piece at a time. His body is warm and bronze, hard with muscle and discipline. In contrast, mine is soft, pale, trembling with need.

The contrast feels electric.

I trace the lines of his chest, his back, the ridges of strength I've only imagined. He shivers under my touch. Boldly, I reach for him, too, with both hands, rubbing and stroking the rigid length between my palms.

When he finally enters me, it's slow and tender, a stretch that steals my breath. He holds still, forehead pressed to mine, waiting.

"Okay?" he whispers.

"Yes," I whisper back, wrapping my legs around his hips, taking him deeper into me.

He moves carefully, each thrust measured, as if he's determined not to break me. But soon his control melts into hunger, and the rhythm deepens. Our bodies find a pace that feels like waves—rolling, building, crashing.

I cling to him, nails in his back, gasping with every surge. He groans into my ear, muttering my name, growling and groaning as he comes apart in my arms.

It's not just sex.

It's choosing life again, together, in the dark of a seaside hotel.

When release finally takes me, it rips through me like a tidal wave.

He follows, holding me tightly, as if I'll drift away if he doesn't.

"Meera," he murmurs into my ear as we both ease down from the high of our shared pleasure. "Stay. Stay with me."

"Yes," I answer. "Yes."

～

Early morning light seeps slowly into the room, soft and tinged with gray.

I wake up curled against his chest, his arm heavy around me, protective even in sleep.

For one suspended breath, I fear he'll be gone when I blink. But when I stir, he does too, eyes opening, warm and unguarded.

"Good morning," he rasps.

Relief and something wilder flood me. I smile broadly. "Good morning."

"You stayed," he says, smiling back.

I prop myself up over his chest, nuzzling my nose against his. "Of course I stayed."

His thumb strokes my cheek in slow, lingering circles. Then he glances toward the pale blush of dawn outside the window.

"We've been chasing sunsets," he murmurs. "Chasing ghosts. Maybe it's time to try something else."

I frown slightly. "Like what?"

His lips curve with something almost shy. "What if we watched the sunrise together instead? A new day. A new start."

A lump rises in my throat, but it's not grief. Tears slip free anyway, soft and grateful.

"Yes," I answer. "I'd like that very much."

He kisses me tenderly then, his fingers gently brushing away my tears.

It feels like a promise.

It feels like a chance at something new.

And when we step out to the balcony hand in hand, the horizon blooms with light.

Not in farewell, but in welcome.

# ABOUT THE AUTHOR

Shirley Siaton writes edgy and evocative novels and poems. Her worlds are in a deliciously dark cross-section of the romance, neo-noir, action, contemporary, and fantasy genres. Her background in various Asian martial arts inspires a lot of her work.

She has several books of fiction and poetry released since February 2023. Her first book is the free verse collection *Black Cat and other poems*. *Befallen* (March 2025) is her first full-length novel. She also pens juvenile literature as Shirley Parabia.

She is an award-winning writer, poet, and journalist in English, Filipino, and Hiligaynon. Her essays, short stories, and poems have been published internationally in print and digital media. Her multi-lingual plays have been staged in the Philippines.

Shirley is a black belt in Shotokan Karate and an international certified fitness coach. She has a Master's degree in Public Administration and works in education, wellness, and publishing. Originally from Iloilo City, she lives in the Middle East with her husband and two daughters.

# ON THE WEB

*Shirley's official website:*
**shirleysiaton.com**

*Complete reading guide:*
**shirley.pub**

*Subscribe to Shirley's VIP list for free exclusive updates:*
**newsletter.shirleysiaton.com**